Eminent Domain

The Iowa Short Fiction Award

Prize money for the award is provided by

a grant from the Iowa Arts Council

Eminent Domain

D A N O' B R I E N

CROWN PUBLISHERS, INC.

NEW YORK

Some of these stories have previously appeared, in a slightly altered form, in the *Denver Quarterly, Four Quarters, Michigan Quarterly Review, Mid American Review, Prairie Schooner, Redbook, South Dakota Review,* and *Sunday Clothes.*

Published by Crown Publishers, Inc., 201 East 50th Street, New York, New York 10022. This edition is published by arrangement with University of Iowa Press.

CROWN is a trademark of Crown Publishers, Inc.

Manufactured in the United States of America

Library of Congress Cataloging-in-Publication Data

O'Brien, Dan, 1947–
Eminent domain.
Contents: Winter cat—Cowboy on the Concord Bridge—Seals—[etc.]
I. Title.
PS3565.B665E4   1987   813'.54   86-30846

ISBN 0-517-57550-7

10   9   8   7   6   5   4   3   2   1

First Crown Edition

TO THE MEMORY OF WILLIAM H. O'BRIEN

Contents

Winter Cat

My dad and I lived alone. I never really knew my mother. To me she was just a dark-haired lady who occasionally towered over my bed late at night. Sometimes I would hear her laugh in the next room. Sometimes I would hear her raise her voice or cry. I've never known enough about her to sort the good from the bad. The only concrete thing I ever knew about my mother is that she lived in North Dakota. Once, not long after she left, I found a map and located North Dakota. I was too young and my eyes fixed on the town of Fargo, a spot on the map far from my dad and me.

We lived on the outskirts of Hector, Minnesota. My friends at school wondered what it was like to live without a mother. They wanted it to be bad. But it wasn't. My dad and I had everything we needed. We had a white house and five acres of land. Between the trees we had built the sheds and in the sheds we raised the birds. We both loved birds and from the very beginning we dreamed of turning our little five acres into a game-bird farm. My dad said that birds were the most perfect thing in nature. We wanted to have the best game-bird farm in the world.

The first pair of birds that we got were pheasants. We collected the eggs and incubated them and in no time we had a hundred pheasants. Then we got bobwhite quail and partridge. We raised lots of them too. It came easy for us. We worked together and by the time I was in the seventh grade people were writing and calling us, asking how we did it. Our secret was simple. We really cared about the birds. That made them feel right and so they would breed for us. We did better than anyone. Together we did things that nobody had ever done with wild birds. The greatest thing we ever did was to raise sharp-tail grouse in captivity.

You see, sharp-tail grouse are delicate, sensitive birds and are hard to keep alive. Dad called them fragile. That was his favorite word for sharp-tail grouse, fragile. He would say it like a church word, like he was talking about the world's rarest piece of glass. Fragile, as if to say it any other way could kill a grouse or make it disappear. He said they were more gentle than quail and pheasants, that they didn't compromise their ways as easily and that was why nobody had ever been able to raise them in captivity. I remember the first one we got. A friend brought it from the prairie somewhere. She had been shot in the wing and kept in a burlap sack for three days without food or water. She was almost dead, with the wound green and the whole bird smelling like grass clippings that have been in the sun. Even with the three days and the wound she was wild as a fresh-caught squirrel. There was blood on the wing, dried hard and dark. She came out of the sack with eyes perfectly round and so black that the light showed crystal in them. She stood for an instant, the tiny feathers on her head standing up like a little headdress. Her neck stretched out to full length as she got her bearings. Then she exploded, beating the broken wing along with the good one and only getting a foot off the ground. She made tight little flips over and over until my father caught her carefully in a towel and took her to a special darkened cage. When he came back he smiled at me. "They're so fragile," he said.

"Will she live?" I asked.

"We'll make her live." He put his arm around my shoulder and then he said, "And she'll lay eggs for us. And when we get a male the eggs will be fertile and then we'll have little grouse." He squeezed my shoulder. "What should we name her?" he asked.

It took me only a second. "Dakota," I said. "She's from the prairie. Her name should be Dakota."

Dad leaned down and hugged me and I could feel the roughness of his cheek and smell the thick, wonderful after-shave that was part of him. "The next thing we do," my dad said, "is get a male." I nodded my head. "Nothing on earth should live without a mate," he said. I looked at him, wondering what he meant. But he was looking at Dakota and smiling.

From that day on Dakota was our most prized possession. I would watch her for hours every day. We kept a clipboard to write down things that she did. Nobody had ever studied sharp-tail grouse before and we wanted to learn all we could. The most important thing, my dad told me, was not to scare her. Other people who had sharp-tails in captivity had found that they could die of nervousness.

Dakota lived all summer without any sign of being nervous. My dad and I took turns watching her and sometimes we would sit together in the summer evenings with her. It was about then that people began to hear we had a sharp-tail that was adjusting to captivity. We began to get letters from game-bird breeders telling of their experience, asking how we'd done it, congratulating us, and wishing us luck with breeding. Some even had sharp-tail grouse and offered to trade them to us. They thought they were impossible to breed in captivity, but we knew better.

It was great fun to go to the mailbox and find letters from different places. Most of them were addressed to the farm. That meant that the people were writing to me as much as to my dad. I would leave the letters on the kitchen table and my dad would open them when he got home. One day, after school had started in the fall, I picked up the mail when I got off the bus. There was the usual bundle of papers and bills, but in the center was a very official-looking letter from the Department of Wildlife in Lincoln, Nebraska. I knew my father had written to several places trying to find a male grouse. One of the letters had been to Nebraska to see if we could go out and trap a male grouse, and so I was out of my head with excitement. I ran to the house, through the back door, and tossed the mail on the table. I wanted to get upstairs to change into my work clothes as fast as possible. But when the bundle of mail hit the table it scattered and a letter that I hadn't seen before slid out and skidded to a stop in the center of the table, all alone. I looked at the letter. It was a small envelope, not a full-sized one like the one from Nebraska. It was addressed to my dad and written by hand. The handwriting was neat, the letters all perfectly formed. It was impossible to tell if it was a man's writing or a woman's. There was no return address. But the stamp was postmarked Fargo, North Dakota. I slid the letter back into the pile and went up to change my clothes.

I kept trying to think of the letter from Nebraska. I kept trying to hope that it said we could go trap a mate for Dakota. But the other letter kept taking over in my mind. I hurried through the chores. I fed every bird and watered them. Dakota was tame by then and looked at me like she could understand. I told her about the letter from Nebraska. "Those letters Dad wrote might be paying off," I told her. "How would you like a boyfriend from Nebraska?" She looked at me and made the little feathers on the top of her head come up into a crown. She clucked. It was as if she was listening. "Eat your grit," I said, and she clucked at me again.

The letter from Nebraska was a permit. It said we could come and trap a mate for Dakota. We were both happy but I couldn't stop thinking about the other letter. We went into Hector for a hamburger. It was like a celebration. We talked about our trip to Nebraska. We decided to go over Thanksgiving, planned what kind of traps to use and how to transport the male grouse home. I was interested in the trip but I wanted to talk about my mother. I'd never wanted to talk about her before, but now I did. Dad talked on about how we should take care of the bird once we got it home and I listened. He talked steadily, which was rare for him, and all the time it was like there was a pressure building in me. In a way I didn't want to say anything, but in the car on the way home it just came out. "Why'd Mom leave?" I had spoken too loud and at a moment when Dad had been quiet. It sounded like I'd screamed it. There was silence afterward, but the pressure was gone. I sat in the dark car and listened for Dad to answer.

It took a long time but finally he said, "I really don't know," and I thought that was all he had to say. The pressure began to build again, but he went on. "She really wasn't mad." He paused and I knew he was thinking back. "She said she just had to leave. She said some women just weren't cut out to be wives and mothers." He shook his head. "I think we scared her," he said. "Something came between us and neither your mom nor I had the sense to fight it."

The car rolled on through the darkness toward the farm. The pressure was gone. I could feel my dad's uneasiness. I thought of the letter for a little while but by then we were home. The huge cottonwoods on either side of our driveway loomed above us in the dark. They formed a tunnel for the car and we slipped in without another word.

I didn't think about that letter again until a couple of days after we were back from Nebraska. We had caught the male grouse that we had gone after. His name was Bruno. He was big and strong and very nervous. When we got him into his cage my dad shook his head. "He's a tough one, isn't he?" I agreed. "Maybe we'd be better off with an old bird that's been in captivity," he said. Then he shook his head. "No," he said, "we'll go with Bruno." He explained that Dakota had been sick when we got her, which had kept her quiet until she had healed, and by then she was tame. Bruno was healthy. He would be hard to tame. The days that followed were filled with taking care of Dakota and Bruno, and so Dad probably didn't think I even noticed the second letter from Fargo. But I did. I saw it there among the other letters, same size, same handwriting on the outside.

We didn't talk about the letters, and my dad didn't let on that anything was bothering him. All day long he acted normally, but at night I knew that he was staying up long after I was in bed, sitting at the kitchen table drinking coffee. One night I came down the stairs a little ways, to where I could see into the kitchen. He sat on one of the wooden chairs smoking his pipe and looking at a book. A cup of coffee sat on the table. I watched him for a long time. I noticed the pipe wasn't lit. He looked older to me, different somehow, not really like my dad. I studied him and tried to figure out what was wrong. At first I thought the kitchen was too big and cold, then it came to me. My dad was lonely.

I crept back up the stairs and got into bed. I lay in the dark and thought of all the other times he had sat alone in the kitchen after I had gone to sleep and I wondered if he had just gotten lonely or if he'd been this way all along and I'd been too dumb to notice.

The breeding season was coming up. We put the birds on artificial light so they would breed earlier. That was my dad's idea. He seemed to always know just what would work, and like so often before, he was right. By the first of January Dakota was acting differently. Bruno, although he was very nervous and flew into the side of the cage sometimes, was starting to act differently too. By the time the third letter came, Dakota had a clutch of ten eggs.

Then things began to happen too fast. The eggs began to hatch and we became the first people to ever raise sharp-tail grouse in captivity. Another letter came from Fargo. A big yellow cat began hanging around our place. The winter became unusually cold. And one day, after all ten of the eggs had hatched, my dad found Bruno dead in his cage.

I had never seen my dad so upset. He came carrying Bruno into the house, the bird's mottled breast upright and tears running down my dad's face. It was very cold. Bruno was nearly stiff. My dad shook his head. "He must have flown into the wire. His neck is broken." I was crying then too. We'd worked for years. Now Bruno was dead and our future rested with ten tiny chicks and Dakota.

That was when Dad decided to go away for a couple of days. He almost never went away but when he did the neighbor would come over and help me do the chores. This time my dad wouldn't tell me where he was going. He'd never done anything like that before. My dad always told me everything, but for some reason he didn't want me to know where he was going. It bothered me a lot more than I let on. I couldn't think of any place he would go and not tell me.

When I asked he smiled at me as if he was happy to be going, but he wouldn't say where. All he'd say was "With a little luck I'll be bringing back a surprise for you." Then he turned away and looked out the kitchen window. He went rigid. "Damn," he said. Without turning back toward me he said, "Sneak out the front door. Get the rifle out of the feedshed." I knew then that he could see the cat from the window. "Hurry," he said.

I moved as fast as I could, out the front door, around the garden, and into the feedshed. I got the rifle and ran back. By then Dad was looking out the back door that was cracked open. "There it is," Dad said, and I handed the rifle toward him. He shook his head. "No, you try it." I almost dropped the rifle in my excitement. "Hurry, it's moving," my dad said.

But by the time I got the rifle up to my shoulder the cat was gone. "Damn," I said. My dad laughed and slapped me on the back.

"You'll get it next time," he said. And by then I had forgotten about asking where he was going, and what he hoped to bring back.

Two days before he left the neighbor called up. "Talked with your dad yesterday," he said. "Suppose you'll be needing some help."

I played dumb. "Help for what?"

"Well, your dad's going out of town, isn't he?"

"Gee, I don't know. Where'd he say he was going?"

"North Dakota," the neighbor said. "Some little town outside Fargo."

I couldn't think of anything to say then. I held the phone to my ear and the neighbor kept on talking but I didn't really hear him. All I remember thinking was that I should have known. I should have known. Finally I said, "No, it's okay. I can do the chores myself." I didn't want anyone else around. I could do the chores myself, I didn't need any help.

When I told my dad that I'd told the neighbor he didn't have to come over, my dad smiled. "That's fine," he said. "You're right, you can handle this place." And we stood staring at each other.

Finally I asked him, "Where are you going, Dad?"

He smiled and shook his head. "It's a secret," he said, and winked. "But when you find out, you'll be glad." Then he went on talking as if that was all he had to say about it. "You know what to do around here. Now, it's going to be cold so be sure the chicks stay warm and if you get a chance, take care of that cat." He walked to the window and looked out. He'd forgotten about my question already. "That cat worries me," he said. Then he turned. "But you can handle it." He squeezed my shoulder and messed up my hair. I loved being that close to him. I loved the smell of him and so I had to smile.

He left Thursday night. Friday morning I fed the birds before I went to school. When I got back I checked to be sure that the heaters all worked and that all the birds had water and were all bright-eyed and looking healthy. It was very cold but I sat with the sharp-tail grouse for a while anyway. Dakota sat fluffed up in her cage against the wall. The chicks moved under the heat lamp in the center of the floor. Around the lamp, we had built a three-foot-high wooden wall. It was warm in their little area and the ten chicks looked happy. I wondered if any of them were males and, if they were, if they would be old enough to breed with Dakota that year. If they weren't we would lose a year. In a way they were our hope.

I looked all around the shed where the grouse were before I started back to the house. Everything was in order. I shut the door tight and latched it. When I turned toward the house a movement drew my attention to a space between two of the big trees in the yard. The old yellow cat moved silently across the opening and behind a tree. I was only a few feet from the feedshed and so I moved over and opened the door slowly. Behind the door was the rifle. I picked it up and slid a cartridge into the chamber. I closed the door slowly and looked to where the cat had been. If I could kill it I would sleep better that night. It would be good to show my dad that I had killed it. I moved slowly across the frozen yard to where I'd last seen it. But when I got to where I could see behind the tree it was gone. I stood staring at where I was sure the cat would be and suddenly there was a movement behind me. I turned just in time to see the cat disappear into a row of bushes. Somehow it had gotten behind me. It gave me the creeps.

In Minnesota the winters are cold. That night was a bad one. When I went out at ten o'clock to make sure everything was all right, I looked at the thermometer and it was nineteen below zero. I took my father's coat from the hook. It smelled like him and kept the cold out. The snow crunched double loud under my feet. The batteries in the little flashlight were weak and finally I turned it off. The night was still and clear, like cold nights always are, and the moon gave me enough light to find the shed door.

It was frozen shut. I kicked at it with the toe of my frozen boot. When the door was free I opened it and the light and warmth from the heat lamp hit me. I moved in closer to the sharp-tail chicks. They all stood under the light, as close to each other as they could get. They were warm under the lamp. I stood shivering, picking up only a tiny bit of heat from the lamp. The light hung in the center of the shed and left the corners in darkness. Against the wall Dakota huddled in her cage. The moon shone white through the door I had left open. When I first came in I didn't notice, but in a while I began to get the feeling you get when someone or something is watching you. I looked into the corners of the shed, but it was too dark. When I reached into the coat pocket for the flashlight a silhouette moved at the edge of my vision. And then the cat, silent and yellow-gray, slipped unhurried across the moonlit doorway and was gone. I remember feeling the heat from the lamp go cold against my skin and then I was wondering if I'd really seen it or just imagined it. But when I went to the doorway and looked down at the tracks, I could see that it had been the cat and that it had to have been in the shed watching me. It was colder then than before. I shut the door and latched it, kicked snow back up against the bottom. I knew the cat would kill the chicks if it could, and I knew that I couldn't let that happen. They were our hope for next year. They were the greatest thing we'd ever done.

I found an older set of tracks and followed them. The tracks went to the back of the shed and came from across the yard. I knew I had to find out how the cat had gotten in and fix it. I looked hard with the worn-out flashlight and finally I found a hole right at the bottom of the shed, not as big as a softball, but big enough for a cat. In the feedshed I found a burlap sack and stuffed it into the hole. Then I covered the hole with snow and packed it tight.

Back in the house I ran increasingly warmer water over my frozen fingers. Slowly the feeling came back. It was midnight when I went to bed. I lay watching the moonlight against the ceiling. The next day was Saturday; Dad would be home tomorrow afternoon. I wondered for a moment what he was doing at that very moment, but I pushed it out of my mind.

Just as I started to sleep the thought of Dakota came into my head. That delicate, fragile grouse with the feathers standing straight up on her head and Dad and I sitting with her every day when I'd get back from school and late into the night. I remembered the books and letters and special cages and the big smile on my father's face when he brought the first egg out and held it to the light and found that it was fertile. Then I could see him checking the incubator, the humidity, the temperature, the alarm, every three hours, all night. Then I felt the pain in his eyes as he carried Bruno into the house, dead. Then I saw the chicks as they hatched, the tiny feathers at their wing tips, and then I saw the cat slipping silently across the doorway and I couldn't sleep.

I was up again at four o'clock. It was colder still. The air seemed sharp and brittle against my face, like broken glass hung suspended in our backyard. It was twenty-nine below zero. I wrapped my scarf around my face to give the air a chance to warm up before it got to my lungs. The shed door was frozen again but I kicked it open. When I saw the chicks the scarf dropped from around my face and my breath came out solid, snapping transparent when it hit the heat from the lamp above the chicks. Five of the chicks lay out away from the light. They were still, frozen where the cat had left them. The other five chicks huddled even closer to the heat.

The old flashlight shone yellow against the white snow as I carried the traps around to the hole that the cat had dug clear. I could see the soft round tracks in the snow, uniform and in a straight line where the cat had crept to the hole and through. Then the line where it had made its escape. Tears had frozen on my cheeks and I felt tired. I wanted to go back into the house and get into my warm bed and pretend it hadn't happened. But I couldn't. I had to fight. I set the traps, one against the shed wall on either side of the hole and one square in the middle of the hole. I blew the powdery crystals over them until they became invisible. The cat couldn't kill the rest of the chicks. It would have to step in a trap first. My cheeks actually felt hard from the cold, but I didn't go into the house. In an hour it would be light and begin to warm up. I sat shaking on the porch, holding a baseball bat to finish the cat if it got caught.

You can hear everything on cold Minnesota nights. The slightest sound cracks across Minnesota snow like a rifleshot across water. I didn't think about the cold. I concentrated on whatever noise the night might send me. I expected a crisp snarl, a scream, perhaps the clank of the trap chain as the cat hit the end. But nothing like that came.

I had been there I guess forty-five minutes when the very faintest of sounds came sharply to me from the shed. I listened, heard it again, and headed toward the shed. The flashlight was so weak now that it was almost useless. The first trap was empty; the cat would be in the one set in the hole.

But it wasn't. I stood above the trap thinking that I must have imagined the sound, then the beam of the old flashlight fell on the tiny portion of snow concealing the trap trigger and I could see that in the direct center was a perfectly round cat track. The trigger had frozen and the trap had failed to work. Suddenly I was colder than I'd ever been before. I heard the noise again, it was the panic of the chicks inside the shed. When I stood up my legs hardly worked. But I ran fast, with the dying yellow light dancing against the shed wall.

When I came to the door my breath was coming hard and I had to hold my scarf up over my face. I still held the baseball bat. I expected to see the cat standing under the light, but it wasn't there. The chicks it had not killed the first time were now dead, scattered around their enclosure in small, soft lumps of feathers. It was as if someone had knocked the wind out of me. I felt sick and again I thought of giving up, but the cat was in the shed and I had to find it. I pointed the flashlight into one corner. The weak light shone just enough to tell me that the cat wasn't there. Then I thought of Dakota. I swung the light into the corner where her cage was and there, one paw through the wire of Dakota's cage, pinning her against the back wall, crouched the yellow cat.

Our eyes met and locked. The cat tightened its grip on Dakota and I could see that it had already taken feathers off her back and neck. She struggled but the five needle claws of the cat cut and held her. I came slow and steady, letting my scarf drop and the bat go higher. The cat raked its claws back and Dakota slumped to the bottom of her cage. The cat wasn't moving. It was staring as if trying to decide whether to attack or run. Then I was close enough to swing. But when I did the cat leaped high into the air. I swung again. Another leap and into the shadows. I swung again and again but my bat found nothing solid. When I turned I saw the cat, standing calmly in the doorway. I stopped swinging, stared at the cat, and then with all my might I flung the bat. It whipped through the frozen air and caught the cat across its back legs. There was a snarl and then the doorway was empty. I turned to see if Dakota was still alive.

She was. I picked her up quickly and unzipped Dad's coat. I held her against my chest and hurried for the house. My fingers were frozen and I struggled to open the back door. When I finally got inside the house I didn't feel warm. I opened the oven door and turned it on before I brought Dakota out from under my coat. She was still alive. I found a small wire cage on the back porch and put her inside. I put it as close to the heat of the stove as I dared. I rubbed my hands together but still could not feel them. Dakota lay on her side, motionless, but her eyes, black as ever, were open and I could see that she was looking around. I sat with her until the sun was up. She did not move.

All day long she lay there. Finally in the afternoon I took her from the cage and held her to the warm part of my neck. I could feel her breathing and moving to get comfortable against my neck. I could feel the tears creeping down my face. I was exhausted and fell asleep.

I don't know how long I'd been there in the kitchen with Dakota against my neck when Dad found me. He must have been able to tell the whole story by just looking at me. I could cry no more. My eyes hurt as I looked up at him. He stood over me, his hat and coat still on and a wooden box under his left arm. He put the box down and took Dakota from me. I was afraid she was dead but she wasn't. He put her in the cage and I could see she was standing up.

Then I was confused. Happy about Dakota and scared to know what my Dad had brought from North Dakota. I looked past him to the door but it was shut against the Minnesota winter. Then I looked at him and he knelt down beside me and smiled.

"Look here," he said, and held the wooden box up so I could peek into a hole in the top. I could barely move but I did what he said. I leaned over and looked into the box. It was dark, but in a little while my eye adjusted to the light and

I could see, crouched in the corner, wild and proud and fragile, an adult male grouse.

"I brought Dakota a boyfriend from North Dakota," he said. "An old man heard about us and offered to give him to us." He tried to say more but he didn't get the chance. I reached out to him and we pulled each other in and held tight. I buried my head against his shoulder and found a few more tears. I breathed in the smell of him and squeezed with all my might.

And that spring we did it again. We did what no one else had ever done. We raised sharp-tail grouse and this time the chicks lived. They grew proud as their parents and the yellow cat that had been indestructible that cold Minnesota night died from a single rifleshot. My dad saw it that spring, sneaking among the trees behind the house. His eyes caught mine and he motioned toward the trees. I looked and when I saw the cat I froze. My dad got the rifle from the shed and came up behind me. He started to hand the rifle to me but when he saw my face he stopped and raised the rifle to his shoulder.

The cat didn't leap into the air the way I thought it would. The rifle went off and the cat lay down and died. We walked over and looked at it. My dad didn't pay much attention to the cat but slapped me on the back and smiled. I didn't feel Dad slap me on the back. I looked down at the cat and saw the scar across its back legs. Finally, I had to know. I leaned down and touched it to be sure that it was real.

Cowboy on the
Concord Bridge

Nebraska. Backwater expanses of grain and pasture, and sweaty men making hay for a winter that will come and kill the land. And since I've known this land I've known that there is a tear in the muscles of my stomach. The tear came from lifting bales of hay that were too heavy, and it nags at me every hour of every day. When I lift things now I know that the tear is getting worse and I wonder why this land produces cubes of grass that weigh so much.

My torn muscles are not a secret. Everyone knows now, but no one mentions them. They have their own. And like mine they do not show. They are under the skin in this land. But there is no hiding them once you've admitted that they are there. Only if you pretend that they're not there will people not notice.

They are the only thing that Tracey missed about me the first time she laid eyes on me. That was Omaha, a night to howl, a good long breath at the surface. She stopped at the Holiday Inn on her way through from California and saw me there drinking Grain Belt beer, one of the hot spots. And she wasn't pretty, not one that would stand out in a crowd, but she did. And I went to her, my restlessness like static sparks across the barroom floor. And she, a Massachusetts girl, seemed a fine excuse.

A fuzzy dream. I remember the talk of her home, inside, factory work. Different dangers. The ocean, forests, people, and cities. All that night and the next morning I listened. I stayed sober, cut the jokes, and listened. And she said things that I had always hoped were real. A glimpse through a door that I had never seen before. But a tiny glimpse, she passed on through and left me in a parking lot, feeling like mallards, north too soon, ponds all frozen.

Poor land. The center of a continent. As far from the ocean, where the rain begins in summer and the warmth goes to in winter, as a land can be. It is a big country that makes men feel small. There are no fences and the cattle mingle. So every year, like the grass turning green, there is a roundup.

Women handle the branding irons and do the vaccinating. My father oversees it all. He's like a part of the land, a butte, a knoll, a solitary gnarled cottonwood. He's always there, watching, expecting the world, same expression no matter what he thinks.

The cows, confused, lowing gently, soft sweet vapor coming from their mouths, follow their calves out. The rope is tight, the calves bawl and buck. The women turn the cows back and descend on the calves with red-hot branding irons and hypodermic syringes. "Bull calf," they shout and Dad walks to where we hold the calf, stretched out, immobile.

"Glad you made it back," he said. Standing tall above me he pulled a whetstone from his back pocket and drew the blade of his pocketknife across it. "Ought to finish today." He knelt down between the calf's legs. We were on the same level then. "We'll just keep at it," he said softly. Smoke from burning hair came between us, and the calf, wanting to struggle, tightened in my hands. It began to bawl.

Dad took a firm hold of the calf's scrotum and neatly sliced off the very bottom. The testicles began to retreat but he caught them in his left hand, pulled them down and cut the cords.

"Nice crop this year." He slapped the calf's rump. "Hope we stay lucky through the summer." We turned the calf loose then. It trotted back to its searching mother.

When I stood up the torn stomach muscles tightened. I felt at them under my belt, wondered if I had hurt them even more. And as I stood dusty in the corral, feeling the muscles and looking out to the green and growing ocean of grass, I thought of Massachusetts. A forgotten land under the sea, paradise on a distant star, and Tracey my starship.

Standing there in the corral, the flatness crashing in on me, I remembered the address smashed between pictures and credit cards in my billfold. I remembered that address and I thought of the summer to come and the winter like the last summer and winter before.

At supper Dad sat cold with a sandstone face. I had told him. Leaving the ranch. East. And I sat enduring his stare. His thin, oiled-back hair, the porous, deep-brown skin. And I knew skin like that came not from the sun but from the wind and cold on the prairie, and from something inside. There would be no faces like that in Massachusetts.

He tried to make me stay with his tiredness. And I squirmed under the eyes that see beneath the surface. Squirmed like a boy, panic poking at me from the corners of the room and an uneasiness, knowing that he would not explain the pain behind those eyes. Knowing that the stare was muscle, blood, and sweat, focused through forty years, and that it all came to a needle point inches behind my own eyes.

So I took the bus from Omaha. Dirty city streets in the middle of America. Black men walking up and down in an Indian's land and the hard gray double ribbon under the bus connecting me to every inch of everywhere. Humming across Iowa. A prairie with corn. Then Illinois and thicker corn and traffic and smoke to the north of the road. Then Gary, Toledo, Cleveland, Buffalo, Albany, and Boston. And through it all never noticing, until I stepped out of the bus and touched one, that there were trees. More and more each mile. And I had thought only that the sky was getting smaller. Then she was there, smiling, a stranger really. And we made our way, sightseeing, snapshooting. Pictures of the city, the Commons, the Charles River, Cambridge, Harvard, and out toward the hills of Massachusetts. To Lexington and Concord. I stood on the bridge at Concord, smiling, one boot on the rail. Tracey, clinging to the eroding bank below, snapped the picture. Then, winding north, we passed the colonial-fronted hamburger joints, maple syrup stands, patched cornfields, and into the timberland. "Miss me?" she asked. "Sure."

In Massachusetts there is a furniture factory like no place in Nebraska. There are trees and hills and a stream behind. The building stands straight in a land of curves. The roof is black. Tar paper. And the windowless walls galvanized sheet metal, not shiny, stained, long rusty tails from every nail head. The ends of the building are loading docks. We watched that first day, from beside a mountain of kindling wood. Whole trees were gaffed, dragged into the building, and at the other end tandem trailers were backed up to the dock. Into their hollowness crate after crate of hardwood tables and straight-backed chairs. Tracey pinched my arm. "There you go," she said. Her round, bright face looked up at me. "Go win that bread." And I walked to the door marked Office.

Sawdust sloped in the corners like cobwebs. An old lady with bifocals chained around her neck sat behind the desk. "Help you?" she asked.

"Yes."

"Job?" She pushed a sheet of paper at me. An application.

Then came a man, Mr. Jenkins. "How long you plan to stay?" he asked. I told him I didn't know. He nodded. "When can you start?"

"Right away."

"Now?"

I shrugged. "Follow me," he said. And we walked through a door and into the whining plant.

Machines. Sawing, shaping, smoothing wood. No one looked up. They watched the whirring blades in front of them. Jenkins switched off a machine. "Maggie Fleming," he said, pointing. A small woman standing between the machine and a pile of rough-cut planks. Jenkins slapped the machine. "The planer," he said. "Listen to Maggie, she knows it inside out." I looked at her then. Her face was cut with deep, dusty wrinkles. She smiled. A grandmother.

There was a T-shirt Tracey wore to a party, D.K.D.Y. written black across its front. Braless breasts between the letters and the people, her friends, new to me, asking what the letters stood for. She wouldn't tell and after twice, my jaw tightened. I promised myself I wouldn't ask again. But she looked at me and raised her eyebrows, then looked down at the letters and took deep breaths, until, finally, late, I asked again.

"What's it mean?" I said and could see that she was not going to tell.

"Don't know, do you," she said and laughed.

"Come on," I said. "What's it mean?"

She laughed again, seemed happy but said, "Don't know, do you," and I could feel my face flush. I walked away.

In our bedroom, as the T-shirt came off after the party, alone, I asked again. "What's it mean?"

She said simply, "Don't know, do you," and wanting it back before it landed, I watched my fist flash out, hitting firmly on the cheek. In slow motion, the wince, the distortion of flesh, and even now the face spins away from me, twisting down, and I can see her looking up, frightened, lip sliced, blood running into her mouth. And trying for New England courage, but appearing as if the taste of the blood pleased her, she smiled.

The rough planks hit the planer's spinning blades and screamed. Scream at us, squeezing rockers from their hearts. I watched Maggie feed the machine. I piled planed boards for her, helped pull stubborn ones from my side. Knots would make them stick in the plane and Maggie would push at them. She would beat on them and finally they would go through, coming out on my side, slightly darker in a stripe where the blades had chewed at the knot.

"Most important thing is keep your mind on what you're doing," Maggie said. "You line her up, straight as you can, and push slow till the blades take ahold. If they get stuck give them a good whack with the heel of your hand. Look in there," she said and pointed into the plane.

I bent down to her level. I could see rough planks through the plane. "Watch," she said and turned off the machine. The spinning slowed and I began to see the blades. Finally they stopped. Shining top and bottom, long and silver, sharp as knives, they blocked my view.

I brought my lunch, ate with Maggie, talking on the steps of the loading dock in the shade of sheet metal. Living trees standing quiet around the factory yard. "Been here fifteen years," Maggie said. "Started on the plane, never thought I'd finish on it. But now I just hope I make it." She winked like a man. I tried to see her behind the wink. "Not a bad job," she said. "Person could do worse." She looked into her lunch pail, rubbed her nose. "Me, I got a garden I've been neglecting too long."

Wine from a party in my head. Lying naked on an oaken bed that Tracey said her great-grandfather had made, I watched the hay fields growing heavy with bales in my mind. And I could see my father, his world spinning around him, feeling a handful of soil and watching the Nebraska sky. The bed, made before Nebraska was a state, pushed up uneven at me. I felt the mattress give. Tracey sat on the edge of the bed. She sat silent. I watched her through half-open eyes, imagining more light, her knees held up tight to her chin, arms wrapped around the legs. She stared expressionless, wide-eyed, not ready for sleep. I touched her. Her hand slid down, touched mine. "Do you love me?" she asked.

"Sure," I said. She looked down at me. Then swung her legs over the edge of the bed, stood up. I rolled, facing the light as it snapped on.

"I've got something to tell you," she said. She stood face away from me. She played with the envelope of pictures on the dressing table. "You're not the first," she said. I touched my temples. "A man named Paul moved out a week before you got here."

I got up. Naked, suddenly feeling silly, I stood in the middle of Tracey's apartment. I stepped up behind her, held her shoulders. She shuffled the pictures on the dressing table. I watched the pictures, Boston, Harvard, Concord, in the mirror in front of us, then put my head gently down against her back, holding her shoulders tightly.

"It doesn't matter," I said. I could feel her body warming. Then a quiet laugh. I raised my head, watched her in the mirror. She was looking at a picture, smiling, the tiny white scar on her lip reflecting back at me. She turned, and tossed the picture back on the dressing table. She put her arms around my neck. Over her shoulder the picture spun on the dresser and stopped. The picture, me, grinning from the Concord Bridge. I put my arms around her waist and she buried her face against my shoulder.

Maggie's last week of work. Talking proudly, nervous, about what she would do when she was done, like she had won a victory. Tracey at home wanting me there, and Jenkins, everywhere, all the time, walking the factory floor, watching. And when I'd turn I would know that I had just missed his eyes.

Finally I didn't look, endured the pressure at the back of my head. Until he stopped me at the time clock. "Think you can handle the planer?" he asked. I told him sure, I could handle it. And his eyes ran up and down my body quickly. He punched my shoulder. A man from here, where the snow falls straight down and lies waist high in the forest, rough face but pale, big hands, steel forearms. Then, as if we'd been waiting, we heard it together. The squeal of the plane cutting a knot. The sound we heard every day, but hearing it now above the other sounds. We turned and went toward it. Just in time to see Maggie's old gray eyes projecting frustration, her hand striking at the plank stuck in the machine. Then the clunking noise and her looking through us both, her mouth screaming. No sound. Her hand being mangled, the plank passing through. She stood an instant, stuck in the machine, then fell to the floor. And my stomach muscles tightened. Blood on everything and Jenkins telling me, "Pick her up. Bring her to the office."

And from nowhere there were people. The ones that I had never noticed, sitting silent behind the machines, part of the machines. They stood in a tightening circle and I shook my head. First time ever, I said, "No." Mumbled it. "No, my guts are torn. I can't carry her." Shaking my head and looking down. Clearly this time, "No." And my voice carried to every corner of the earth that I will ever set foot on.

"Pick her up," Jenkins said. But I only stood, holding my stomach. The long, gray faces of the others pressing in on me. Black eyes, the chant. Pick her up. And me, in the center, shaking my head, thinking I should not be there. And I knew my father, storm clouds at his back and a handful of dirt in his fist, was staring across the land with his dust-bowl eyes. And I turned and ran. Pushing the people, amazed how strong they were, through the plant, burst into the morning air, and ran on, away from that place. Away from the people and the trees. And realizing, almost immediately, that all of it would haunt me. Even in Nebraska, for the rest of my life.

Seals

For two weeks Jarret has dreamed of seals: buoyant, nearly transparent, floating on the tops of the black waves of the North Pacific. And even now, standing at the bar below Effie's Place, in Kenai, Alaska, he cannot get them out of his head.

His partner is upstairs with one of the girls. It is the last night of their four days off. In six hours they are supposed to be at the airport to meet the single-engine Cessna that will take them back to work. There is gin in his glass but he is not enjoying it. He is thinking about the next ten days, about pushing heavy Alaskan soil with a bulldozer. And he is thinking back.

That crazy Bob, he thinks. Walked right up to a girl with someone else's arm around her and asked if she was open for business. Jarret swigs the gin and forces a smile, but he cannot sustain it. In fact, the smile lasts only a few seconds, and though he knows that no one in the bar notices him, he feels someone is watching. Seals, he thinks, and leans forward with his elbows on the bar. The big shoulders hunch up. He can still feel the icy salt spray coming over the bow of the boat, and so he swivels around, putting his back to the bar and the salt spray. The people in the bar are mostly oil men, oil or construction for oil. Alaska is filled with them. They are what his mother would have called lost souls. He wonders if his mother would be able to recognize him if she walked through the door at that moment.

He and Bob had come up the Danali highway two years ago. They hadn't really wanted to end up in Alaska but they had felt a need to see the world, to get out of Des Moines.

Iowa. It seems a billion miles away. But his family lives there. And Bob's, and everything else he knows for sure. Iowa drifts in and out of his consciousness. The black dirt and cornfields, the small towns and slow warm rivers move easily in and out. But now all of it is watched by the seals.

They'd signed on as roustabouts, made enough money to go moose hunting that first fall and make it easily through the winter. They'd hung around Anchorage and gone out with a couple of women. Then that next summer they'd gotten jobs operating bulldozers above the Brookes Range. The money was even better and the summer passed quickly.

The second winter was cold, and that ate on him and made the time pass slowly. The cold was more brittle than Iowa's. But the worst part was the darkness. It was like a dream. It was like knowing you should be asleep because it was dark outside but really being awake and moving around like it was day and finally not knowing whether you were awake or sleeping a familiar dream.

And sometimes it was like a nightmare. By the end of February everyone in the bars in Anchorage got mean. The money was running low and the summer and jobs were still a couple of months off. Outside it was cold and still. And very dark, day and night.

Jarret watches the people in the bar. From across the room he can see a huge horsefly buzzing in lazy circles. He watches it moving along the far wall. It lands for an instant on a dried-up palm tree beside the window. When it moves again its flight is short. It comes to rest on the shoulder of a big man sitting alone, the man whose arm had been around the girl Bob is upstairs with. The man freezes but lets his eyes shift toward the fly. He wears heavy logging boots and a dirty cap with ALASKA written across the front. The fly is enormous and Jarret can see it moving on the man's shoulder. Then, too quickly for Jarret to see, one of the big hands comes up and clamps down on the fly. The big man gathers the fly into his hand and shakes his fist to be sure that the fly is caught. With the other hand he reaches out and peels a long piece of palm leaf away from the plant in the window. The man hunches over and becomes intent on the fly and the piece of palm leaf. Jarret cannot see what he is doing and his mind wanders to this summer job and the lousy construction camp across Cook Inlet from Kenai, and finally to Bob and his crackpot idea to go seal hunting.

"It's not the time of year to hunt seals," he'd told Bob.

"So what. This is the last frontier. You been complaining all spring about going into town on our days off and blowing our paychecks. Here's your chance to save some bucks. We can stay out here for nothing. We borrow a boat from the Indians and go up the inlet and do some seal hunting."

"I'm not much on water," Jarret said.

"Hell, we used to swim in the Des Moines River," laughed Bob.

"This inlet is a little colder. They say you only last a couple of minutes in there."

"Hell, the Lord hates a coward," Bob said and laughed again. The laugh bounced off the scrub trees that lined the shore and went dead as it dispersed across the water of the inlet.

"I never shot a seal," Jarret said.

"Me neither," said Bob. "It's about time. They call them the wolves of the water," he said.

Jarret hears Bob and turns to see him coming down the stairs. His right arm is around the girl. Jarret orders a bourbon and soda for Bob as he stands at the bottom of the stairs whispering into the girl's ear. He watches Bob and has to smile. Bob is the same way he had been back in Des Moines. Then Jarret's mental map of the USA becomes vivid and he realizes for the thousandth time how far Des Moines is from the ocean.

Even though Jarret's eyes are open he can see the map clearly. He stares at it and doesn't hear the labored buzzing noise until the horsefly has circled his head twice. Then he sees the movement from the corner of his eye and instinctively jerks sideways. The shape of the thing disorients him and before he can realize what it is, his fists are up in front of his face. It is the horsefly he had seen earlier. But now a six-inch strip of palm leaf has been inserted in its anus.

Jarret reaches out and plucks the exhausted fly from the air. The fly struggles in his hand, but after the palm leaf is removed it is able to fly away. When he glances at the logger he expects him to be smiling. But the logger isn't smiling. He sits rigidly, his heavy neck and jaw tense, and stares blankly at nothing.

"You'd only last a couple of minutes," Bob kept saying as they started out. "Some of the highest tides in the world," he said.

"Now look, we don't know anything about boats so don't go fucking around." Jarret had heard the thin tone in his own voice. "This thing looks like it's lucky to be afloat," he said.

"No sweat," Bob said. "The Indian gave me this." He tossed a coffee can into the front of the boat, and smiled. "Just in case she leaks."

They loaded extra gas for the outboard, the food they'd taken from the cookshack, an old shotgun, and a box of shells. It was a beautiful day, fairly warm, no wind. The water was calm and the air clear enough that you could see an oil platform ten miles into the inlet. The tide was going out.

The tide, Jarret thinks. In Des Moines a tide was something that lapped on the beaches in movies and in the lyrics of songs. How were they to know that in Alaska tides could roar, could twist steel beams like coat hangers.

Bob slaps him on the back. "I feel better," he says. He picks up the drink Jarret has ordered without saying thanks.

"That means you'll be ready to climb back into that airplane for ten more days of pushing Alaska into different shapes?"

Bob closes his eyes and shakes his head. He lets his lips go loose and moans. "I'll be ready," he says. They both look out at the barroom. A couple of girls circulate among the tables. Some of the men smile and joke with them but most are busy with their own conversations: bulldozers, drilling tables, bits, nets, next fall's moose hunt. A few are thinking private thoughts. They sit alone, the way Jarret had been, with a drink somewhere close, the ice melting, condensation gathering on the outside.

The girl Bob had been with walks by. Bob reaches out and catches her arm. "Don't forget my change," he says.

She smiles and twists her shoulders away from his grip. "I thought it was a tip," she says.

"Bullshit," Bob says, but the girl is gone.

Jarret laughs. "She owes you change?"

"I gave her a fifty. I got twenty bucks coming."

Jarret laughs. "Forget it. What's twenty bucks?"

Bob shakes his head. "Nothing," he says and pushes himself away from the bar. He goes to the men's room. Jarret moves away from the bar too and goes to the window. It's ten-thirty at night but it's still light outside. It's almost as bad as the darkness of winter. He's never gotten used to walking out of a bar, ready for bed, into a world that is light. The parking lot is full of pickups and old cars. Their old Chevy is parked with its dented door toward the bar. It isn't much. They'd bought it in Anchorage, just to get them down to Kenai, then parked it at the airport to use on their days off. The camp wasn't far by plane but it was still remote. There was no way in or out except by plane or boat. The flight took only twenty-five minutes and made the fifty-mile-wide inlet seem like just a river or lake.

But the inlet is something very different. Jarret knows that now. He pictures it as the mouth of the North American continent, a mouth sucking water, a mouth breathing the Pacific Ocean in and out. In and out, according to the moon. In and out, walls of water with each slow breath.

Like remembering a woman or a bad horse, he thinks first of the beauty. The hum of the outboard motor on the small wooden boat made it unreal from the start. Jarret sees it now as if he were above it. They cruised along the shoreline, a tiny speck on that water, moving slowly toward the mouth of the Tyonek River, thirty-five miles up the inlet.

Bob sat in the back steering and Jarret sat in the front. The old shotgun leaned against the seat between them. They watched the water of Cook Inlet and the scrub conifers along the shore. Occasionally they passed the tent of an Aleut fisherman. Salmon nets hung like huge leaden cobwebs on poles. In front of the tent an old wooden boat, like the one they were in, was pulled up onto the beach. Only once did they see a human: an old man, standing on a rock, staring out motionlessly. They waved but he did not wave back.

It took them four hours to reach the Tyonek, and when they did they didn't recognize it. On the old map they had found in the foreman's trailer, the Tyonek was a thin blue line starting somewhere in the mountains to the west. When they came to it, they had thought it was a bay, or that the inlet jogged to the right. But then they saw the whitish-brown water mixing with the blue-green of the inlet and they knew that this huge, flat expanse of water was the Tyonek.

Suddenly they were in a maze of submerged islands and sandbars. It was the Tyonek River delta. The water washed cold and milky-thick over and around the sandbars, then rushed into the inlet. The river, at its mouth, was a full mile wide. It churned and eddied in a thousand separate rivers, and when Jarret put his hand into the water he could feel the glacier that it had been only days before.

"According to the Indian, the seals should be around here," said Bob as he steered carefully toward where the river narrowed and deepened.

Now Bob is moving around the bar. Jarret notices the big man with the ALASKA cap watching him. Bob is laughing loudly and spilling his drink as he talks to two drillers. The big man drinks alone and glares at Bob as if repelled by his good humor.

Jarret moves toward Bob. He puts his arm around Bob's shoulder and gives him a solid squeeze. "Let me buy you a drink," he says.

Bob looks at Jarret, starts to protest, then gives in and goes with Jarret to the bar. "I don't really need you to buy me a drink, but I'll buy you one." Bob smiles. He reaches into his pocket and brings out a single dollar bill. "Maybe I can't buy you one. I still didn't get my change back."

"Kiss that twenty bucks good-bye, buddy."

The bartender puts the drinks down and Jarret pays for them. When he looks into the glass of gin he sees the ice rocking back and forth and sees a tiny seal head between the cubes. He shakes his eyes clear. He knows that he is not drunk, he knows there is no seal in his glass. But that was just the way they'd looked. Heads were all he saw.

"There," Bob had shouted, and from reflex Jarret had raised the gun to his shoulder and fired. The pellets hit the water exactly where the seal's head had been, but it was impossible to tell if it had been hit or not. Bob revved the engine and in seconds they were peering down into the cloudy water where the head had been, seeing nothing.

"Maybe they don't float," Bob said.

"Maybe I just missed it," Jarret said.

Another head popped up in the center of the river. It was too far to shoot but Bob pointed the boat toward it and they moved slowly. When Jarret thought they were close enough he fired again and they sped toward the spot. And again they found nothing but swirling white water.

"I had him in the sights," Jarret said.

"You might have got him," Bob said. "We got to get there faster."

Now, in Kenai, Jarret can't believe that he did those things. He can't believe that he'd shot at something that he wasn't sure he could retrieve. But he'd done it. Urged on by Bob he'd shot almost a whole box of shells at seal heads. They had raced from one bank of the river to the other, shooting wildly at one after another.

It had been a kind of frenzy. Something to do with being a man in Alaska. The frontier frame of mind, oblivious to everything, especially to what was happening around them. While they plowed the water of the Tyonek River the earth was going about her business. She had positioned herself so that the moon slid over the continent of Asia and released its hold on the Pacific Ocean. The tide had begun to return. And, while they had raced madly after seal mirages, black clouds had gathered to the west, over the headwaters of the Tyonek. They hadn't noticed.

Had they been seals themselves, or moose such as those that had watched them, unseen now for hours, they would have felt it, smelled it in the air. But they were neither seals nor moose. And so they were surprised when the wind began to foul the surface of the river with ripples as if a thousand silent shotguns had sprayed their shot across the water. Then the light, the sun itself, went bad. Jarret can remember raising his head from the stock of the old gun and feeling a chill. When he looked around, the world had changed. And when he looked at Bob he could see that he too had felt it.

"I'm going to get my twenty bucks," Bob is saying. "Twenty bucks is twenty bucks and she didn't come near earning it."

Jarret wants to stop him from pushing away from the bar, to tell him to forget it. But the feeling of earth change is still with him. "Be careful" is all he can say.

The delta was gone when they got to the mouth of the Tyonek. And the inlet, God, the inlet flowed now with its own force. It had become a river itself, fifty miles wide, sucking its water back from the moon, filling itself with the Pacific Ocean. The confluence was a whirlpool. The old wooden boat was driven by the river water and the wind that blew, harder now, from the shore toward the center of the inlet. There was no chance of turning the boat before they hit the whirlpool. The old boat rose up on the swell and slid down across the twisting water. The wind pushed them through and suddenly they were no longer in the river. They were in the inlet. What, with the tide out, had been a flat, peaceful body of water was now moving darkly, the milk of the river gone, with an irresistible current rushing toward the heart of Alaska. The ocean was moving quickly into the mouth of the continent. The water caught and held the tiny boat. The outboard could just hold its own. It could not move against the force of the tide.

Jarret tried to measure their movement against the shore. But nothing moved except the water below them. He felt stationary in a flowing world. He felt invisible. But they were not stationary. The wind was across their beam, hitting them broadside, driving them out into the frigid water of Cook Inlet.

There was nothing to do except hold their course for home and be taken out further from shore. The waves from the tide and the wind quartered against the wooden hull of the old boat, and with every impact water squirted from the nail holes on the right side of the boat. Jarret looked back at Bob standing in the back of the boat, holding the course as best he could, drenched with salt spray, grim-faced. The man in the boat did not look like Bob. He bent over slowly and picked up the coffee can, tossed it into the water at Jarret's feet. "Bail," he said with his eyes.

And so Jarret bailed. He let every other thought slip from his mind and bailed. If he didn't slow down he could keep up with the water that came in through the nail holes and over the sides as the waves hit. But if he slowed at all the water gained on him. So he put his head down and refused to look at the waves that crashed harder now against the fragile planks of the boat. On his knees in the water in the bottom of the boat, his fears concentrated themselves into acute perceptions: the sound of the can scraping the bottom of the boat could be heard over the crash of the waves and the whistle of the wind. The water squirted from the nail holes in slow motion. Once, when Jarret looked, he saw the last point of land disappear. And still the water came, and the wind, and Jarret felt that he could not keep up much longer. The last time he looked up he saw a seal head riding peacefully on a deadly black wave that hung above them. The seal was only a few feet away and Jarret's eyes locked with its shiny black eyes. Jarret couldn't stand the seal's gentle gaze. He looked away, to the dirty cold water in the bottom of the boat, and he prayed. For the first time in years, he prayed. He told God that he was sorry, told Him he had done so many things wrong, told Him that if he got to shore again he would leave Alaska forever. He begged God to save him. And then he bailed. He bailed until his strength was gone.

The sky was dark and very cold when the tide stopped coming in. Both men pretended not to notice. They were afraid to hope. But slowly, almost imperceptibly, the tiny boat began to move. It pushed through the waves. It made forward progress. In an hour they saw land. In another hour they were nearing shore. When they reached it the old man they had passed earlier that day stood again on the rock looking out to sea. They called out to him but he didn't answer. They moved on past.

By the time they beached the boat at the construction camp they were talking and laughing. The talk didn't make much sense and the laughter was nervous and strained. But it was laughter and they were thankful for that.

Jarret is brought back to the present by the sound of Bob's voice. "Open up, damn it."

Bob is standing outside the women's restroom and pounding on the door. The big logger with the ALASKA hat has come off his chair and is moving toward him. Jarret puts his drink down and steps to intercept him. Both men are halfway across the floor when Bob stops yelling. The last thing he says is, "Okay, bitch, you asked for it."

Jarret moves quickly but not quickly enough. Bob's foot hits the door just beside the knob and it pops open neatly. The girl is sitting on the toilet counting money. She had thought she was safe and now her mouth comes open in a long, high scream. Somehow there are swear words within the scream and as Bob snatches the bills from her hands she makes a swipe at his face. The long fingernails seem to miss, but as Bob plucks a twenty from the stack of bills there are three lines of blood on his cheek. He tosses the rest of the bills back at her. Jarret has gotten there too late to stop the logger and when Bob turns, his face is met squarely with a fist.

Then Jarret is in the middle of it. He hits the logger hard on the back of the head with his fist as he goes into the restroom after Bob. The girl is standing now, trying to stomp on Bob's head with her high heels, but the logger knocks her down as he reels from Jarret's rabbit punch. Jarret reaches past them both and takes Bob's arm. He jerks him to his feet and they start for the door. They are running when the cool air and light hit them and Jarret curses the midnight sun as he helps Bob into the Chevy. He hears yelling from the barroom doors and knows that it's all right. That they will not be chased. When the car starts, Bob begins to laugh. He says something about getting his twenty bucks. Jarret glances at him and sees him laughing through the blood in his mouth and on his face. Jarret doesn't laugh. He pushes the accelerator to the floor and they spray gravel against the building.

They gain speed as they leave town. They are going eighty when they pass the road that leads to the airport. Bob stops laughing.

"Hey," he says, "that was our turn. You're heading for Anchorage."

Jarret pushes the accelerator even harder. "No," he says, "I'm heading for Iowa."

Eminent Domain
A Love Story

You can say a lot of things to a woman, but don't ever tell her not to let the door hit her in the ass on the way out, because she won't. She'll be gone before that door has a chance to slam and she won't be back until long after the sound of that slam has stopped ringing in your ears.

Willy Herbeck can be the meanest, most insensitive son of a bitch the world has ever seen. He's dirty, sloppy, unsociable, old-fashioned, moody, bullheaded, and ugly. But he's got class. I guess that's why I married him in the first place, and that's why I moved out on him, too. He's got an independent orneriness and when he takes a liking to something he doesn't care what other people think, he sticks by what he's said come hell or goddamned high water.

That's why when I heard that the state highway department had been out to buy the place and Willy had told them to get out, I knew we were in for trouble. Willy, I said, it's a fair price. You haven't sold fifty dollars worth of parts off this place since spring and here they're offering you ten thousand dollars. He just sat there and read the newspaper. They'll get it, I said, the law says you have to sell. Bullshit, he said.

He hadn't even read the letters we'd sent him. I figured he was confused or maybe couldn't read so I went out and offered him top dollar right off the bat. They said he was a funny, hard-to-deal-with kind of guy, so I thought, hell, give him the ten grand, move those junk cars out of the way, and save everyone a lot of problems. He said that there were one hundred and thirteen of them and they weren't for sale, and I tried to explain that he had to sell, that the highway was coming through and that there really wasn't much choice. Then he grabbed me by the arm and led me back to my car and put me in and said good-bye.

So I was stuck. It's my job to get the land that the department needs and I don't get much time. I went and looked up his wife.

They told me she was young and good-looking and worked in a cafe at the intersection of Route 50 and Route 27. I asked for Shirley and the girl smiles and says she'll send her over. She brings me a cup of coffee and I wait. When Shirley comes I can't believe it's true. She's about thirty-five, blonde, nice body, white teeth. That slob of a junk man must have something going for him. The guy had to be fifteen years older than she was, he was dirty, rotten teeth. I looked her over real good, figured there had to be something wrong with her; but if there was, I didn't see it.

I told her what I wanted. Said that Willy had practically thrown me off the place and she should have a talk with him. It's a good price, I said, and let me give you a little inside scoop, the state ain't going any higher. She said she didn't think Willy would sell and I explained to her that he'd have to eventually. She nodded and asked if I needed anything. I said I was all set and as she walked away I wondered why a gal like her was with a guy like Willy Herbeck.

I did like the state man said, because he was right. I tried to talk Willy into selling the place. He was lying under the '48 Dodge in the front yard and I was trying to talk to him. Willy, I said, you can't fight them. They'll come and take it and put you in jail, that's what will happen. He didn't say a word. Keep it up then, I said, be a pighead. He said nothing. I kicked the Dodge, and that brought him out. You listening to me, I asked. Not much, he said. Well you better start listening to me, you're messing with the state, I said and pointed my finger at him. He looked back at me and said, Shirley, don't kick this car. It's a driver. Driver my ass, I said. They were all drivers; just needs a fan belt, he'd say, or a new wheel. They were all drivers, all precious pieces of junk and the truth is none of them were ever drivers. They all just sat and the people would come with good money and try to buy parts and Willy would just say, no, he didn't have it, and the people can see the thing they came for hanging off one of those junk cars and Willy pretends like he's never seen what they're looking for and tells them to get off the place. Now the state was offering him ten thousand dollars for the whole place and he was acting like they were someone who came looking for a gas cap.

Threatening and puffing up your chest is a waste of time. Nobody ever proved a thing in a pushing match, and nobody ever held onto nothing by talking about it.

After dinner he started going in and out of the house, carrying little boxes of things and kind of keeping them hidden from me. I was watching television and trying to ignore him. Finally he quit coming and going and sat down in his chair to watch television. What was all that about, I asked. Nothing, he said. Come on, Willy, I said, I know you're up to something, what was in those boxes? A little of this, a little of that, he said. I could see that he wasn't going to tell me what he was doing so I just ignored him again. But the longer I sat there the madder I got. I'd been living with him for a long time and I'd been bringing in the money ever since the first and now that he had a chance at ten thousand dollars he wouldn't even talk about it. And then he starts sneaking stuff out of the house. I couldn't stand it.

I screamed. Willy, what are you going to do about the state, and what was in those boxes? I yelled a while longer and finally he says, I guess I'll have to fight. And the second he said that I knew he was serious and I knew that those boxes were filled with supplies. Where'd you take those boxes, I asked, and he answered exactly what I knew he'd answer. I took them up to the '26 Packard, he said.

I've been buying land for the state for a long time and I don't think I ever had one like Willy Herbeck. He must be a mean bastard. He even threw that good-looking gal out of the house for trying to convince him that we were offering him a good deal. I talked to her the day after she got thrown out and she said she didn't care if she ever saw him again.

I went out again, hoping that maybe he'd thought it over and changed his mind. I was kidding myself, he was too mean to give in to anything. I knocked on the door and nobody came. I cleaned the dust off the window and looked in. Didn't look like anyone had ever lived there. I walked around to the back. There were car parts everywhere. Cracked engine blocks, old batteries, differentials, transmissions, fenders, hub-caps, junk scattered everywhere.

Behind the house the land rose to what must have been a little hilltop. You couldn't see any ground, nothing but wrecked cars, and nothing new, all old, rusting, smashed cars. I glanced over them all, then hollered to see if anyone was around. There was no answer. As I turned back toward the house I noticed a license plate leaning up against the house. I could see it was an old one. I reached out to inspect it and inches from my outstretched hand the siding on the house shattered, pieces of wood splintered, and I heard the rifle shot. I hit the ground behind an engine block. A voice boomed out from above, GET OUT. I looked up, and this time saw a person sitting behind the wheel of the Packard at the top of the hill.

They say that stainless steel is the best material to put bodies in for burial. When I die, I want them to cremate me, and put the ashes into a Stanley thermos bottle (they're stainless steel), and put the bottle in the glove compartment of the '26 Packard and not tell anybody where I'm at.

They came to see me at work and I told the sheriff, husband or not, I was staying out of it. The sheriff looked over his shoulder at the state man. He took a shot at this man, Shirley, now that's against the law and you gotta do something, he said. No, sheriff, I don't have to do anything, I said. The sheriff turned and led the state man into the corner of the cafe, I went on cleaning the counter. They were back in a minute. This time the state man was doing the talking.

He started off with, Mrs. Herbeck, I know that you're upset about all this and I know that when the state is forced to take over property that there are often serious adjustments to be made. I folded my arms across my chest and listened to him. You and your husband have had a falling out, he said. That's understandable, it's a trying situation. But, he said, and smiled slyly, this is not the time to alienate your husband. This is when he needs you most. Then he winked, and the time that you need him most.

I thought for a second. Okay, I said, I'll talk to him. He touched me on the shoulder and said, now you're thinking straight. He motioned to the sheriff and the three of us drove out to the place to talk to Willy.

When the sheriff stepped out of the car three shots hit the ground in front of him. He leaped back and said he was going to call the Highway Patrol. I told him not to do anything and got out of the car. They both yelled at me to get back but I didn't pay any attention, I knew Willy wouldn't shoot, and I knew right where to find him.

He was sitting in the driver's side of the Packard, peering out of the side window over his rifle barrel. Hold it right there, he said. Hold it yourself, I said, and walked over to the Packard. I looked into the backseat and could see that it was full of food and ammunition. What the hell do you think you're doing, I asked. I thought you weren't coming back, he said. So I'm back for a minute, I said, what the hell are you doing? Nothing, he said.

I took a good look at him sitting there in that old Packard, the backseat full of food and ammunition and the tires all flat. He was dead serious. You think you're protecting this place, I asked. He wiggled his mouth around under his nose and I knew that meant that he figured he was. Well, you're nuts, I said, you aren't protecting anything. You're just making a fool out of yourself. He rubbed the black stubble on his chin. That don't much matter, he said. I could see that there was no sense in even trying to talk him down from the hill. I kicked the Packard. You're a fool, I said, they'll shoot you dead as hell. He'd been staring down the hill toward the sheriff and the state man but raised his eyes to look at me. Don't kick the '26, he said, she's a driver.

He didn't listen to his wife the first time but I still thought he might. Something had to be done, the superintendent was starting to breathe down my neck. The sheriff said he'd give him a week, then go up and get him. Every day the sheriff and I would spend hours at the junkyard, every evening I'd stop at the cafe and talk to Shirley.

Once or twice a day the sheriff would call up through his megaphone, WILLY, YOU'RE GOING TO HAVE TO COME DOWN HERE AND TALK. THE STATE MAN IS HERE AND HE'S WILLING TO NE- GOTIATE. But Willy would not come down. And every time that Willy didn't answer the sheriff's message the sheriff would say, he left, he must have just deserted the whole thing, and the sheriff would step out from behind his car and smile. Then shots would ring out from the top of the hill of junk and the sheriff would jump back behind his car, grab the megaphone and say, WILLY, YOU SON OF A BITCH.

I kept telling Shirley that the ten thousand would be her ticket out of the junkyard. She's a smart gal, she knew what I was saying but played dumb. She kept talking about what was the best way to handle Willy, but she was smelling her share of the money and what she was thinking was what was the best way to get that in the bank. I told her that if she talked him into the ten thousand that she'd be doing herself a favor, that she'd earned it, and I was telling the truth.

If she could just get him to take the cash, she could get her share and get the hell out of there. I'd seen it work before. A guy like Willy could drink himself to death with five grand

and a gal like Shirley could get a fresh start. It's a fact of life and Shirley knew her facts of life.

Somewhere there ought to be a law that says you don't have to sell what you got just because someone offers you a good price for it. There ought to be a law that everything isn't for sale, and people should realize that happy is happy and when you got it you got it. Everybody should think about that, especially women.

I kept thinking about Willy up there in the Packard, fighting his little war for no reason, and all the time I was figuring, ten thousand dollars divided by one hundred and thirteen cars in the lot is eighty-eight dollars and forty cents per car. And that's a lot more than they're worth. At first I just got mad when I thought of it. There he was, king of the mountain. But this wasn't a game, it was for real. The sheriff wasn't kidding and it wasn't right that Willy was playing with my life in his game. After all, there wouldn't be a mountain of junk to fight over if it weren't for me. Willy didn't have the ambition to support himself over the years it took to collect all that. In a way that mountain was half mine. I began to hope that the whole thing would just be over.

On the Wednesday after the Thursday when the sheriff had said he'd give Willy another week, the sheriff and the state man paid me another visit. He's still up there, the sheriff said, he shot at me twice today. Now tomorrow we're going up there and get him out, and we won't be pulling our punches. This is about your last chance to talk him down. He talked like he meant it, and I could see that the state man was serious, too. Will you give it another try, Shirley, the state man said, it's in your best interest. I untied my apron. Yeah, I said, I'll try again.

So five minutes later I was walking up that hill toward Willy and the Packard and I was thinking again about all those years of supporting Willy and I could remember them by the heaps of junk I passed. The '57 Chevy with the mashed-in left side had come in on Christmas Day four years ago. I remembered because Willy left the turkey dinner I'd made to go out and get it. And the '58 Edsel that had been driven off a bridge was there, and the wire-wheeled Hudson from fifteen years before and the blue '62 Ford with the green racing stripe, they were all there. I could see them all and could remember all the screaming and fighting that they had caused, and then I saw Willy sitting in the Packard, his very first car, and before I said anything to him I turned and looked over the junkyard. I saw the view that he had from the Packard. I saw every junker—drivers, he'd call them—and I saw every oily piece of junk that I'd helped him collect. And on the horizon, still miles away, I could see the ink-black exhaust smoke from the bulldozers and earth movers.

When she came down off the hill we asked her what he'd said. She said that he hadn't said anything. Then the sheriff asked her what she'd said and she said, nothing. They hadn't said a word to each other. The sheriff frowned, turned away and kicked at the dirt. Shirley turned to me and asked for a ride back.

In the car, she spoke first. You know, she said, I worked for that business, probably more than Willy. I nodded my head, I could see what she was getting at. I figure, she said, that since Willy can't talk to you, that I should. I nodded again. I'd been wondering when she'd get around to dealing, she was a woman, she could get Willy to do like she wanted, no matter what he wanted. I think, she went on, that I can convince him to take your offer. This time I smiled, it had paid off. She'd put the ultimatum to him and they'd take the money and she'd be wearing new clothes in a week. Good, I said, I knew you could convince him once you saw what was best. But what, I said, would happen if he still says no, if the sheriff has to go up. She turned to me and said simply, they'll have to shoot him. Then she asked me to turn down a side street and told me to stop in front of a wrecking service. Let me out here, she said.

When two people agree to spend their lives together it seems to me that they gotta be able to pick up the slack for each other. When you live with someone you gotta be able to know that her little hands will scrub the inside of the pickle jar when it's empty, if you'll unscrew the lid when it's brand new.

The sheriff was there before the state man and me. There were four squad cars and the deputies stood behind them, wearing helmets and checking their guns. Sheriff, I said, I want to talk to him, I think I can talk him out of a fight. You had your chance yesterday, he said, time for talk is done. But you have to let her try, the state man said, it could save some trouble, maybe even a life. The sheriff frowned. How long, he asked. Ten minutes, I said. Okay.

It was just getting light when I started up. I called out to Willy as I went, to be sure he wouldn't shoot in the half-light. Willy, I yelled, it's Shirley, and my voice bounced in all directions off the gray forms of the junkers. Don't shoot me, I said, and halfway up, beside the '41 Studebaker pickup, I called again. Willy, I said, don't be pointing that gun at me. And this time he called back, shut up, he said. When I came to the Packard I could see him sitting there, his rifle barrel pointing out the window and the bill of his baseball cap pulled down low over his eyes. Hold it, he said, what do you want? They're down there waiting, I said. Yeah, he said, I heard them drive in. They're coming up, I said. It was almost light and I saw him glance in the backseat. Well, he said, I'm almost out of food anyway.

I walked over to the Packard. I got a deal, I said. No, Shirley, he said, I've made up my mind, I'm staying with this junk for the rest of my life, and he smiled and rubbed his nose with a greasy hand. That's the deal, I said. His eyes narrowed and I knew he was listening even though he acted like he wasn't.

I talked to Ray over at Ace Wrecking Service, I said. Willy still wouldn't look toward me. He said he'd move them for us, I said. Willy glanced at me from the corners of his eyes. There are one hundred and thirteen of them, right, I asked. He nodded. At twenty dollars apiece for the move, that's four thousand five hundred and twenty dollars, I said. That leaves us over five thousand dollars to buy another piece of land.

He turned his head and looked at me, then motioned toward the seat beside him. Get in, he said. I climbed over the stack of rusted wheels that lay in front of the Packard and Willy kicked at the passenger's door from the inside until it came open and I sat down. We can pick a new piece of ground, he asked. Sure, I said. He'll move all of them, Willy asked. All of them, I said. And I can supervise, he asked. I don't see why not, I said.

Willy cleared his throat and let the rifle barrel slip onto the floor. It went through a hole in the floorboards. He stretched his oily arm over the back of the front seat and leaned back. A new yard, he said to himself and dangled his left arm over the steering wheel. Maybe somewhere out by the dump, he said, I'd like that. And we looked straight ahead, through the shattered windshield, the sun was coming up bright and we could see the black smoke from the bulldozers just beginning to rise.

The Inheritance

THE INHERITANCE

Now it is time.

There is a young man standing in the woods just where the stream turns and tumbles white through the break in the beaver dam. It is Jim Martin, and he has stood by the old broken ash tree before.

It is time.

Jim watches the eastern sky as the sun flashes over the ridge. It is a needlepoint of light through the low oak branches. It seems so intense, as if it might twinkle like a star, and Jim is amazed that it pulses only once just as it crosses the gap between clumps of oak leaves. He watches, and in minutes it is full and round, leaving the hardwoods behind as it rises. Jim has almost forgotten all of that.

He looks at the rod, runs his fingertips lightly along the lacquered split bamboo, and thinks back to the day when his father, Ace Martin, had given it to him. The sturdy old creel presses against his side and Jim feels that here is everything his father ever gave him. *Here. The sun is up. It is time to fish.* The thought of his inheritance brings a click of Jim's tongue and a shake of his head. He remembers the day Ace gave it to him. His father had never fished again. It was as if he had known about the cancer that was eating him. It was as if, after that day, he'd given up. As if there was nothing more he could do.

Jim stops and stares at the surface of the water. He stands where he can see what's on the surface but where the fish can't see him. He is trying to see if there is some kind of fly the fish are feeding on, something he could imitate. But he sees nothing.

He dips his hand into the creel for a box of flies. He can feel the hog-ring pliers in their special case with the pouch for the brass rings swinging alongside the wicker basket. He has never known what hog-ring pliers were doing attached to a fishing creel. But they were there when the creel had come to him, and he'd never bothered to take them off. He sorts through the fly box until he finds a Royal Coachman and ties it on the line. He looks at it and thinks that the tiny red feather at the tail should bring him luck. He looks again at the water, and still he sees nothing.

But look. Under that rock just where the back eddy from the water coming over the beaver dam slows. See the crack there in the rock floor of the stream? It's a caddis fly cocoon. Isn't it moving unnaturally? Isn't something making it move besides the action of the water? Yes. No question. And stuck to the inside of that sunken willow root. It's another. And yes, it's moving too.

He moves toward the water now in the old patched boots that have hung in the garage for years. They're dry and cracking and won't keep the water out for long. When he steps into the stream he wonders why he has come. It had been childish of him. To stomp out of the house, gathering up the old fishing equipment as he slammed doors and kicked furniture, was something that even one of his children wouldn't do. Now he feels guilty, knowing that Jimmy and Karen must have heard him fighting with Julie as they lay trying to sleep. They had heard too many fights in the night during the last month. He is ashamed. He had put a pressure on his children that no child should have to endure. And as he feels the coldness of the water squeeze his legs, he thinks that his parents never fought. He wonders how that could be.

But he had had to get away from the argument over the job offer and the move to Los Angeles. He imagines that he looked foolish to Julie as she stood at the door watching him throw armloads of gear into the station wagon. "Where are you going?" she had asked.

"Fishing," he had said without looking at her.

She had said nothing, but as he backed away from the house he had glanced up, pretending to be checking that the front of the car did not hit the mailbox, and had seen her leaning comfortably against the doorjamb with a smile on her face and a brightness in her eyes.

So he had driven the fifteen miles to the river in the dark and slept there in the old sleeping bag by the car like he hadn't done for five years. He'd lain there and tried to think of how beautiful the stars were. He'd tried to be moved by the cold night sky and silence around him. But all that had come to him was the promotion. From second in charge of an out-dated New England woolen mill to manager of the new nylon plant in California. It was the chance of a lifetime, a chance to give his family an opportunity, sunlight, to get them out of dark and dying New Hampshire. But Julie had said flatly that she would not move. He lay in his sleeping bag and, at first, felt a suffocation, the frustration threatening to explode. But finally he forced himself not to think about it. And then he began to feel silly again. As the grayness between conscious-ness and sleep came to him, he decided that it was crazy, lying there on the ground in the woods. He almost got up and went home. But sleep pinned him there inside the sleeping bag laid out beside the station wagon. And he slept soundly until just before dawn. He got up as the stars were swinging low on the horizon and came to the old ash tree to watch the sun rise. Now he moves into the deeper water of the stream, and for an instant, excitement rises in his chest. But a chill comes and again he wonders what he is doing there.

There is a thin mist coming off the water and it's warmer there above the water than it was on the bank. Jim strips some line off the old reel and lets the Royal Coachman float along unattended until there is enough line out to make a short cast. He picks the rod tip up and the fly leaves the water with-out a ripple, without dampening the hackles one bit. The back cast is smooth, and when he brings the rod forward the Royal Coachman drops, as if from a bush or branch hanging over the water, just at the edge of the sharp piece of granite that makes the water speed up three feet below the beaver dam. It's as if he'd practiced every day of his life. An observer would never guess that he hadn't made a dozen casts in the last five years. *They might think it was old Ace again, there in the fast water below the beaver dam. But it isn't. It's Jim, the boy. The one who used to come here with Ace and cast nearly as well as the old man but with less effort. Jim, the one who could fish these holes fast and accurately, wade the worst water this little stream has, and finish the day, any day, with a creel full of nice, fifteen-inch rainbows. The one who would look at Ace and his empty creel when they met at the old ash tree in the last warmth of the sun and laugh a little and say, "Where are the fish, Dad?" The one who never knew if Ace was telling the truth when he'd answer, "Still in the stream, son. Got one good one. I knew you'd have supper." No. That man there moving his wrist like it was liquid and dropping the fly exactly where it should be isn't Ace. It couldn't be Ace. Ace never used a dry fly unless he was fooling around.*

Jim watches his dry fly drifting downstream and remembers being a kid in the bait shop, hearing his father speak of dry flies more than once. "One step above a worm," he'd say to the men standing around the stove while the February wind whined at the windows. "Kind of like snagging carp," he'd say and pass the bottle of brandy to the next man.

And finally one of them would have to say, "Phooey, I can catch more with one of Bob's Light Cahill rejects than you can with all the fuzzy wineglass trash on your hat put together." And the man would jerk his head down to show that it was true, then look to the little man sitting behind the thick glasses wrapping the body of a fly with nearly invisible yellow thread. "Ain't that so, Bob?"

The little man would nod but wouldn't look up. "Catch a lot of fish with floaters," he'd say. "But the real big ones usually come in here with a nymph hanging from their jaw." He'd take the fly from the vise and toss it onto a box of a hundred just like it.

"But how many big ones do you see?"

Bob would shake his head, "Not many."

"And a guy catches more fish with a dry fly, right?"

"No," Bob would say, "most fish get caught on a worm." And Ace Martin would throw back his head and laugh a full, brandy-breathed laugh. He'd clap his hands and when his head came back he'd be smiling wide between stubbled cheeks. He'd take the bottle that had made a round. He'd drink and hold the bottle up to make his point. "Something else," he'd say. "You don't see many big ones come through here."

"One or two a year," someone would mumble.

"But that don't mean they ain't getting caught and released." And Ace would take one more swallow through his smile as the others shouted him down.

The ice is gathering in the rod guides now, and it will be tough casting until it warms up. Jim lets the fly float away from him, past the stumps and around the granite rocks as he strips line to it. He'll fish this way down to Falcon Rock. By then it will be warm enough to cast and he can fish back upstream to the beaver dam and have his lunch. Jim gathers in the line, dries the fly by flipping it in the air a few times, clears the guides of ice, and shakes out enough line for a short cast. He rolls his wrist over and the fly floats perfectly into the white water where the stream widens below him. He feeds out the line, steering the fly subtly under the turf of the bank that is eroded from beneath. He knows there should be a trout there.

And there is. It comes up camouflaged by the whiteness of the water at the edge of the hole under the bank. It takes the fly as it comes up, and Jim sets the hook lightly as it disappears. He has forgotten the feel of something alive at the end of thirty feet of line and leader. It is like nothing else on earth, a quiver and quake of pure muscle transmitted lightly to the wrist. Suddenly the voice comes back to him and he is ten years old again. "Feel him, son. Don't haul on him. Feel him." Then, "No slack now. When he wants to go, let him go. If he'll come, bring him closer."

Jim points his rod back over his shoulder and stretches the net down to where the trout will be coming. He holds it still and pulls the tired fish over it. It is a small fish but it's a start for lunch. It's always a disappointment to Jim that the fight doesn't last any longer than it does. He never could make them last like his father could. He used to watch when Ace thought he was alone and even the small ones like the one he is slipping into the creel, which Ace tried not to catch, would fight for five minutes. "Touch them so lightly that they think maybe they aren't caught," he used to say. "It should be a surprise when the net comes up under them."

The boots are starting to leak, and Jim thinks for a minute that he might give it up. He really shouldn't be goofing off like this, he thinks. Skipping work to go fishing was not what had brought him to the attention of the board of directors. But it is warming, and the guides are not so icy. He'll be able to cast again soon and he likes that. He has always been proud of his casting.

From where Jim Martin just caught the little rainbow, the stream cuts sharply to the left, away from the bank where the fish was lying, and drops four or five feet in the next hundred yards. The water is fast there but empties into a large pool cut deep into the granite at the base of a sheer cliff. The cliff is Falcon Rock and the pool below is Falcon Pool. In the bottom of the pool there are more of the cocoons that were stuck to the rocks below the beaver dam. In fact, there are cocoons all along the bottom of the stream for its entire length. But these, the ones below the beaver dam for a quarter of a mile, are moving. There is a door at the end of them, a tiny lid, and these doors, in this stretch of the river, have been sealed now for two weeks. They have been still for two weeks. The very deepest part of Falcon Pool. See the door moving? This one is ahead of the others. It is moving faster than any of them. Look very closely. The door is beginning to crack and shed back from the opening. And look! Small moving tentacles. The pupa is dying. The caddis fly is being born.

Look at it. It's struggling with the door. There, it's broken loose and the current takes the door downstream. Now the fly rests, then begins to test its new body. But it cannot be still for long because there is something it has to do. It wriggles out of its case and feels the current that has lulled it for these last two weeks, but it is no longer comfortable there. It rests a moment longer and then there is a need within and it begins moving wildly. It tries its wings but the water feels wrong. Only movement feels right, and then it releases the bottom of the pool and as the current begins to take it, it becomes clear that it is to fight the current, to struggle upward, and up it goes. Into the current and arching upward. Suddenly the water is lighter and it is the air and sunlight that are lacking. The fly must have the air. It struggles against the current and upward, knowing now that it must break with the water. As it approaches the surface the feeling intensifies and it swims faster. It rises and now the water below it is dark and forebidding. It is the air and the light that it must have. The surface. Closer, closer, and just before it breaks free the water below it explodes, and now the current means nothing. It is sucked into the rainbow's mouth inches from the surface. And from above there is only a tiny eddy as the fish's broad black back swirls the water below the surface and descends again.

But Jim Martin, standing now above Falcon Pool, doesn't see any of this. He has never really understood it. Not even when his father would tell him about it between pulls on his pipe. No, he doesn't see this. But it is happening. The caddis fly hatch is on.

Jim stands resting a moment before he fishes Falcon Pool. He hears the young blue jays chattering nervously in the pines behind him. The pool brings back memories as if the water emptying into it from upstream is lettered with notes and reminders. Ace stood right where you're standing. He'd crawl when he approached the pool. He sat on that little rock there smoking his pipe and watched. Damn, Jim thinks, if I'd known his ghost was wading this stream today I'd have stayed home. *But it's too late now, Jim. The past and your father are all around you. Sit down. Look into the pool. What do you see?*

He sees Falcon Rock, reflected high and jagged in the pool. It rises three hundred feet as if rooted in the stream. It is alone. The now-blue sky seems to be part of it. The puffy clouds move past it as if they had someplace else to be. He'd listened to his father tell about the falcons that had been there before the war and for a few years after. He would always start with, "They are gone now," and look up as if he could still see them. He would take out the pewter flask before he went on, raise it to the sky in a sort of toast, and tip it back. "You don't remember," he'd say to Jim. "Hell, you were just a baby. It was after the war, until about '50. I trained a falcon every year for five or six years, and in the fall we'd kill ducks with it on the ponds south of Baker."

But Jim remembered. Jim knew all about it. The whole town knew. His father quit fishing in September and went to work in the woolen mill, supposedly for the winter. "To build a little nest egg so Mom can quit her job," Ace would say. But when the sun would show bright in October and November, after a gray front had moved through bringing some rain or maybe snow, the foreman at the mill didn't look for Ace Martin. Everyone knew he would not be at work. Everyone knew he would be out in the nipping autumn air, running fast for a man of his age, over the pastures and small grainfields trying to keep the trained falcon in sight as she chased one of the ducks that had come down with the cool weather. He'd do that every day until he'd lose her. Then he'd beg his job back and be sad and depressed for a week to think that she'd leave him. But on one of winter's first mornings, he'd wake up and say to Jim's mother, "You know, Mom, I'll bet she'll be back at the rock next year and maybe raise a brood of her own." He'd smile for the first time since the falcon had gone her own way and Jim's mother would know that Ace had heard the geese passing in the night and she'd know that she could expect a call from the mill, wondering where Ace was that day. But she didn't have to look in the closet to know that Ace's goose gun was gone, too.

And when Ace would talk about the falcons to his son, who had heard it before, he'd look up at the rock and say, "I can't explain what it was like." He was older then and so he'd go ahead and try to explain it. But Jim never understood and his father would always end by looking hard up into the sky above Falcon Rock and saying, "But they're gone now."

Jim could remember the years after 1950 well. Those were the years of the wet black Labs in the front seat of the family car. Those were the years that Ace had somehow gotten ahold of a side-by-side Purdy twelve-gauge shotgun, and he'd sit with the Lab at night oiling the gun and talking about how he hoped it would rain and be miserable, so the ducks would begin to fly. He'd hold the Purdy like it was a baby, raise it to his shoulder, and talk to the dog who had sprung up, hoping he'd shoot. "Sure hope it's snowing up north," he'd say.

But later, when the times were lean, or maybe in a card game, the Purdy disappeared. It was not long afterward that Ace had given Jim the reel and the creel and the rod. By then it was all that was left.

Another rainbow just swirled under the surface, Jim. Jim is looking up at the rock, past it, high into the sky at a speck of dark. *Then watch the speck. It's good that you noticed.* It must be a pigeon, he thinks, riding the updraft off the rock. *Pigeons don't pump their wings like that.* He squints up as the bird flies close to the sun. It's moving a thousand feet above the rock, hanging there as if on a string, waiting for something to happen. Jim is sitting down looking up, and at the corner of his vision he sees the young blue jays chasing each other, bouncing from branch to branch in the pines. He decides that it is time to start fishing again and stands up. *Watch the speck.* The jays have forgotten that he is there, but as he moves they stop their play and sit nervously on the tips of the branches. *Look up. Watch the speck, Jim.* He stands to full height and, just as the jays leave the branches and start off across the pool, he thinks to look back at the speck.

He hasn't focused on it when it flips in midair, so he's not sure that the feeling he has is right. He feels it coming at him. He hasn't noticed it enlarging yet. The twisting and acceleration have not registered with him. All Jim knows when he stands up beside the pool is that he feels everything in the woods go quiet and still. There is no movement except the jays, now awkward over the center of the pool, and the falling speck. For a long time there is no sound. Time is a hush and space means nothing until both are shattered by the eerie, building sound of rushing air, and one of the jays shrieks. At that instant movement redoubles, as if to make up for what it has lost. The jays scatter into the trees on the other side of the pool; there is an audible whack, something black gliding downstream, inches over the water, and nothing is left but tiny blue-gray feathers floating on the surface of the pool and a feeling in Jim Martin's chest. For the first time in his life he experiences the panicky, somehow joyous feeling that something magic has happened.

The only hint is the jay's feathers on the water. A falcon is back, he knows. *But there is more.* He feels a swollen place in him and knows that something more has happened. He looks to the feathers and catches a movement just under the water. A rainbow has just rolled, feeding. Because he doesn't know what else to do and because he knows he must do something, he quickly strips off line and, without any back cast, lays his dry fly just where the rainbow rolled. But the rainbow will have none of it. Now he sees another twist of water and knows that more fish are feeding. He picks the fly up off the water and drops it on the second movement. Nothing happens, and he senses something else under the water and puts the fly there. As he watches the line, there is a roll just under his fly and he realizes that they will never hit his Royal Coachman. There is a hatch coming up and like one more of the notes floating into the pool he hears Ace saying, "Watch the water; it will tell you all you need to know."

And so he stops fishing and watches. *In the shallow part of the pool there is a log almost completely submerged where rainbows lie in the mornings and evenings.* Jim notices a dry stump sticking out of the water. *With the sun past the rock and shining down into the water, it is warm there by the log and the fish have moved to the deeper water, where they are beginning to sense the excitement of the hatch. On the undersurface of the log, two feet underwater, there is a caddis fly cocoon moving rapidly. The cocoon lid has drifted off downstream and the nymph fly is ready to make its dash for the surface. The air is not far above it there in the shallow part of the pool and in a second it is there, floating on the surface. It rests, feeling the swirls of activity there in the deeper water that will build for hours now as the bulk of the flies emerge. It tests its wings, stretching them and causing tiny ripples to spread out in the relatively still water there by the stream's ledge.*

Jim squints his eyes and removes his hat to scratch his head. *Ten feet away in the darkness a wide tail swivels the trout toward the submerged log and flips slowly, moving the fish toward the bank and up. The wings of the caddis fly wave again as the need to mate begins to take over. See the tail speed up as the rush begins? The wings wave again and the fly rises just as the water swells and finally erupts beneath it. The trout passes close, this time out of the water, and causes a turbulence in the air that nearly topples the fly in its first five inches of flight.* Jim's head turns quickly toward the sound of a fish rising. *But the fish misses and the fly rises in jerks to find a mate.* Jim sees a movement just above the twisting water. He watches it, squinting again from the reflected sunlight. *The caddis fly moves four feet off the sur-*

face of the water, gaining agility as it begins to circle the pool. It dips low and, as it climbs, it is recognized and caught in Jim Martin's hat.

Look closely. Know what it is? Jim lets the fly crawl inside his hat and finally onto the brim. He stares at the fly and sees the long tentacles that flare back from its tiny head, where the mouth apparatus is working continually at nothing. There is a fuzziness to the six legs and the back. The front legs point forward and are jointed, almost like a human's arms. The other four legs point backward and remind him of a grasshopper. The wings are transparent and wide. The fly spreads them and slowly lifts from the brim of the hat. He's off to find a mate, Jim thinks, remembering at least that much.

He flips open the tiny box and sorts through the flies. He picks up a Quill Gordon and the name comes to him and he knows that the high, divided wings are to mimic the mayfly. He stares at it, amazed that he recognized it. He lays it back in the box and picks up a Bi-visible and, at once, sees that it would float in any kind of water. The hackles run its full length, and the white hackle in the front would make it stand out even in rapids. Suddenly the box is more than just a mass of feathers tied to hooks. He has to fight the impulse to inspect them all, speculate on their use. But there is no time now. He's looking for something that will imitate the flies that are hatching. Finally he comes to a King's River Caddis and knows it was tied to look like the fly that had crawled onto the brim of his hat. The wings are tied down and are large, the hackles stiff. He takes it from the box and lays it on the brim of the hat. *Yes, it's close. But not the one you want.* As he starts to close the box he notices one more fly. *It's the fly your father would have used.* He looks closely at it. It lies brown and dark in the corner of the box. It is plain and nondescript. He looks at the King's River on the brim of the hat and shuts the lid on the Hare's Ear.

Ace would have sunk the Hare's Ear to the bottom of the

pool and raised it gradually, letting it go with the current like the hatching caddis flies. Jim ties the dry fly on, dabs on some silicon to be sure it floats, and lays it out into the pool. Immediately there is a swirl, but the rainbow lacks interest and misses. Jim fishes the pool completely, dropping the fly all the way around the edge and on every movement he sees. He picks up one small rainbow and a brown before he starts to move back up the stream toward the beaver dam to cook his lunch.

On the way he picks up one more rainbow and that makes four. They are small and he thinks he can eat them all. He is hungry. But more than that, he wants to eat these fish that have just come out of this cold stream. So he gathers wood as he climbs out of the stream at the beaver dam. He leans the rod into the branches of a pine tree and lets the armload of dried wood crash to the ground there under the old ash tree. The fish are already cleaned and in their bed of dried grass at the bottom of the creel. They are small but respectable, Jim thinks. He hangs them each from a green stick he has cut from one of the progeny of the old broken ash. The fire is crackling hot and he forces the fishless end of each stick into the moist earth around the fire. He has brought nothing else to eat. Today it will be only fish. He adjusts the sticks so the trout won't burn and leans back to look at the sky.

And that is maybe good, because it is so much like the water that he will learn by watching it, too. He is thinking of the falcon and the stoop now. He's thinking, maybe I imagined it, maybe it didn't happen at all. But he knows it did. The feeling it has given him embarrasses him. *If he only knew that no one here minds if a man feels like that.* Then he thinks of Julie and the argument that she says is over. "I didn't marry a Los Angeles executive," she told him. "And I didn't want the father of my children to be one either."

"Did you want their father to be a lower-level manager of an obsolete textile mill?" he shouted back.

She looked hard at him then. "Christ, Jim," she said, the tears welling up in her light-brown eyes. "I married what I thought you were, not what I thought you might become."

He closes his eyes and the sun swirls the blackness with red. Twists it and contorts it like molten metal. Stirs it. *Like the water of the stream for a quarter mile each way from the beaver dam. The hatch is progressing. Most of the fish have been aroused. They are feeding now on the caddis flies as they rise to the surface. Soon they will be intoxicated with them and the excitement will grow to a frenzy until the hatch is ended.*

Some of the flies have mated and soon the females will be coming back to the water to deposit their eggs and start the cycle again. When they do, some of them will be taken. But the best fish will ignore them and feed on the swimming flies until they are stuffed.

Jim thinks as he lies back enjoying the sun. First he thinks that he can't let the fish burn, then he thinks about his wife and family. Julie had said he was working too hard, that he should relax. She had even suggested, a time or two, that he go fishing. How was she to know that the memory of his father wouldn't really let him relax? Was that it? Anyway, she was concerned about him. In a way it was like when his mother had been concerned about Ace. They were both concerned about taking care of their men. But Jim refused to take advantage of his wife the way his father had taken advantage of his mother. He wanted the best for her, wanted to leave his children more than he had been left.

Now he is back thinking about his father and he opens his eyes and sits up to turn the fish. And as he takes the fork out of the bottom of the creel he sees the leather-cased hog pliers that were part of his great inheritance, and as he begins to eat he remembers that day when Ace had given them to him. The taste of steaming fish brings the memory clear, and the smell, that smoky succulent odor, breathes life into that day, eight years past, when he and his father sat on that very spot and Ace Martin gave his son everything he had in the world.

Jim was almost twenty-four that day. The trips with his father had become fewer and fewer in the last years, partially because his father was slowing down, dying, they found out later, and partially because Jim was at the age where other things were much more important. He remembers that on that day he had been preoccupied with his job as he is today. He wasn't yet married, but it was in the wind. The family was already planned. He remembers that they had stopped fishing for the day and that he was anxious to start home. But his father had wanted to show him something, and so for fifteen minutes he'd watched as Ace had stood above the water that ran gently into the beaver dam and showed him something about fishing a fly off the bottom. He'd tied on the Hare's Ear and gone through an explanation of what he was doing and exactly why. The demonstration was a rarity, but the explanation was predictable. As always, it was because it looked more like the real thing. But Jim can't remember exactly what it was that he had been shown that day. All he remembers is that one other day he'd sat huddled in his parka trying to keep the rain from soaking him while his father performed the same maneuver.

That day in the rain it hadn't been a lesson. His father had been fishing. They'd been heading home to beat the storm when his father had suddenly stopped and peered into the water. He'd made Jim stop and be still and they'd watched the water together. They had been walking along a deep, swift stretch of stream and Jim could see nothing unusual in the water. But Ace had waved him to get back away from the bank and held his finger to his lips as they moved. When they were ten yards from the stream Ace had looked at Jim quickly, with a smile, as he put the joints of his rod back together. "A hatch is starting," was all he said, and Jim had pulled his collar higher against the rain that was beginning to splatter through the trees. "Not me," he said and sat down at the base of a tree preparing to get wet. Again he couldn't remember exactly what it was that his father had done. All he could picture was Ace there by the bank on his knees with the rain pouring down, casting into the stream, bringing his rod up slowly. He knelt in the mud, his pipe turned upside down, with a broad smile. He'd caught a nice fish that day in the rain, and as he fished he was laughing.

It seemed to Jim that, at least at first, his father was happy on the day of the gift, too. He was maybe a little crazy then and so Jim didn't pay much attention to the lesson at the head of the beaver dam. And when his father had taken the rod apart and put it into its case and handed it to him, Jim thought that it was another of the strange things he had begun to do. "I always wanted my son to have something that was mine," he'd said that day. And Jim had been unable to keep from showing that he pitied this man who could give his son only some old fishing equipment. Ace looked at him and said, "There's more," as if he'd read Jim's mind. "It's . . . ," and he paused as if he was embarrassed or trapped by the words. "It's in a trust," he'd said quickly as he stood up. "I'm going to leave you more than just the gear." He smiled. "You're just not old enough. It's in a trust," and Jim had felt bad for him. He'd looked up at his father that day and, for the first time, thought that his father might be dying and felt ashamed and very sorry for him.

Thinking of that makes Jim feel bad all over. He tosses the stick that the last trout had been baked on into the fire. Then he stands up and kicks dirt over everything. The sun is past midway in the sky. The sadness mixes with the warmth from the sun and seems sweet somehow. It slows him and makes the day seem more valuable. He isn't ready to fish just now so he takes the rod and creel and walks to the edge of the beaver dam and sits down. A chill runs up his back. He looks around into the woods behind him, then back at the water. He stares at the water and his mind empties, first of what might be happening at home, then of his wife and children, then of his mother, and finally of his father. He sits staring deep into the water with nothing going through his mind at all. *Look closer.* He stares for a long time and the trees behind him disappear. The bank he is sitting on is gone. Suddenly there is no air. *Now you can see.*

There is nothing but water. *Look.* And things moving in the water. It starts with the current that comes in over the bulk of the water, skimming over the deep, colder water. A water bug runs upstream on top. Minnows dart along the shallow rocky bottom like horned larks on a winter road. Beyond them there are strange currents, running in layers, cold and warm, performing as the rocks and snags of the bottom dictate, the way gravity, the twist of the earth, and the moon tell them to go. And even more subtle, currents from the things that live in the water at the head of the beaver dam. The tails of fish push the water against itself and the fish forward; there are spinning eddies deep and shallow working on vertical and horizontal axes, three-dimensional whirlpools as the fish spin in place. And Jim can see the flies moving up through it all, trying to go straight up but curving with the main current and being buffeted by the smaller ones, fighting for their lives and for the air that has disappeared for him. The fish, feverish, prey with a lust beyond hunger.

The chill comes to Jim again and he spins around just as the woods reappear and the air whooshes back into his lungs. He stands up staring at the water as if it is a cauldron of evil forces. He takes up the rod as a sort of weapon, and as soon as he feels its warm cork handle, its delicate weight, and the balance he had never realized the reel gave it, the water no longer seems evil. It becomes a kaleidoscope. And Jim Martin knows that the nine feet of bamboo in his hand can twist it into a million different shapes.

He pops open the fly box, where the flies lie all in their place. Each one entices him, shines from the box and attracts him like a gem. The long, silver-bodied bucktails and streamers flash the plumage of grouse and gamecocks at him. The dry-fly hackles stand out straight and bristling. The hair of fox and badger and polar bear and rabbit are all there where they belong in just the right proportion. He runs his hand over them all, thinking of what to use. Finally he sees the fly he wants. In the corner, away from the brightness of the Yellow May, the Fan-winged Coachman, the Orange Dace, and the Mickey Finn, lies the homely Hare's Ear, and the instant Jim sees it he knows it's the one.

He ties the turtle knot slowly. Something is trying to enter his consciousness. He tightens the knot and tries it by holding the Hare's Ear and pulling gently on the leader. This is what was happening the day it rained. His father had been trying to show him how to fish it. He kneels at the water's edge and dips the Hare's Ear in a pool of still water. He dabs it up and down to soak it and it is no longer a dull tangle of rabbit fur. Now it is the caddis nymph. Jim continues to raise it off the bottom of the shallow pool and let it back down. He tries it at different angles, at different speeds, and slowly it begins to be like what he has seen in the beaver dam.

Now you are thinking. To make it look right the fly has to start at the bottom and come up at an angle, as if it's fighting the current but taking the shortest route possible to the surface. He stands up from the little pool with the wet fly hanging from six inches of leader. He is looking at the water. Where would the trout be? *There, against the other bank, under the overhang, out of the sun.* And he strips off ten more feet of line and easily flips the fly upstream from the overhang. That should give it time to sink. And now he waits as the fly sinks and the current brings it to where the trout should be. He tries not to let the line bow and be taken by the faster current in the middle of the stream. The fly must come straight up from the bottom, not be pulled to the center of the stream. He waits there, remembering how his father had raised the rod gently, and he sees now what he was doing.

The Hare's Ear is there now; see it bouncing along the bot-

tom, tumbling over the pebbles in the current. It's on the bottom where the masquerade should start. Pick it up, Jim. Lift it like it's real. Now. Easy, feel how it should be. See, in the shade there. Something moved just when you started up. Easy, it's watching, swinging downstream to intercept you. Look at its wide dark back. It'll come in the last few inches. It's moving in. And the fish sucks in the Hare's Ear with expanding gills and dives for the bottom.

Jim sets the hook an instant late. The initial contact was light and Jim was not ready, but the fish is hooked now and the line whistles from the reel and slices the current in a zigzag lightning bolt across the stream. The fish runs downstream for fifteen feet, then cuts back to Jim's side of the stream. Then it stops and Jim brings in some line so there is no slack. He can feel the fish breathing there at the end of the line, waiting, resting, thinking perhaps, and Jim tests it with a gentle pull on the line. That triggers an explosion. Back into the middle of the stream and toward Jim. Jim is bringing in line as fast as he can but the fish is ahead. Now it has the slack that it needs and breaks off again downstream. With the current behind it, the fish comes to the end of the line. Jim realizes too late that it has changed direction. He doesn't have time to strip line and he sees it go taut, stretch as it brings the fish out of the water, and he sees the hook tear free with a snap as the big fish shakes its head. But the fish hangs there over the water showing the deep color of its side to Jim. The leader piles on itself five feet from where the fish has disappeared, and now all is calm as before.

It is the biggest fish Jim had ever hooked. The best fight by far. Mechanically, he brings in his line, still staring out to where the fish hung suspended over the water. The sun is low in the sky now and with a sudden panic Jim thinks there won't be time to try again in another pool. It was the setting of the hook, he thinks. I set the hook too late. The strike was so light. He clambers up the bank checking the Hare's Ear as he goes. It is in good shape and he moves on upstream. Unconsciously he is thinking that he must get above the next pool, cast even further upstream to give the fly time to sink as it passes him, and then lift it when it is downstream, on the bottom and in sight of the deepest part of the pool. There will be just enough time, he thinks. He looks over his shoulder at the sun.

And then he finds the pool he is looking for. This is it. It is long and wide with only a slight current. In the middle is a huge granite boulder that splits the pool and forces the water to each side. He knows that this is the place. When he sees it, it is like it has happened before. He knows there is a giant fish just behind the boulder. The water is deep but he moves in on his knees to be sure the fish doesn't see him. He sends the fly upstream to begin its descent to the bottom. But it doesn't look right. He picks it out of the water and moves it over a foot toward the center of the stream. He doesn't want to miss the exact spot where the trout is lying. Now he waits as before. Conscious of the tension in the line, trying to imagine just where the fly is in relation to the rock and to the bottom. He brings the rod tip down so it will be ready to begin the ascent. When everything is just right he starts to raise the fly. *Now.*

The fly tumbles into a break in the floor of the stream bottom and moves along the break for three feet. When it appears at the other end of the break, just where the boulder curves up and finally out of the water, it is being lifted from above. But there is no way to know that it is being pulled by an invisible line. It looks now exactly like it is swimming for the surface, coming from the crevice, making its escape from the water. The old trout moves from the deepest, coldest part of the stream with a wave of his tail. He holds himself facing the current and watches the ascending fly. He waves his tail again and moves over a foot and up. He studies the fly. He has been fooled before, but he has seen the flaw in a thousand other flies. He is old and gnarled, his lower jaw grown out and his eyes deep-set in muscly bulk. The current is nothing to him. The tail wags as it has every hour of its long years of life. There is no hurry, there will be no mad rush at this escaping fly. It cannot get away.

The old fish rises above the fly, looking closer yet, then swims slowly to within inches of it. Just as the long, solid black dorsal fin is about to break the surface, the fish waves his tail and takes the fly gently into his mouth. *Not yet.* He gently expels the fly and Jim feels it go in and out, but waits. When the old fish takes it in the second time Jim brings the rod tip up as unhurried as the fish himself and feels it come up solid. There is no great rush and splashing of water. The fish simply swims to the bottom. But the line sings off the reel and Jim knows he's hooked him well. Now the old fish turns and runs along the bottom with the current for more-open water. He swims away from the boulder and heads for a pine tree that has fallen into the tail of the pool. Jim can see the old branches coming out of the water fifty yards away and knows he has to turn the fish. The line is coming off his reel faster than he could strip it himself. The drag is set too loose for this fish, the tackle too light, and Jim can see the backing begin-ning to show under the green line. He takes the line in his hand and squeezes down on it with his thumb and forefinger, trying to slow the fish, trying to give him more to pull, trying to tire him. Jim puts all the pressure on the line he thinks the leader can stand and gradually the fish begins to slow. Then he is lying still in the center of the pool, stopped short of the pine tree. He lies there, and this time Jim waits. *Wait.* He keeps the line firm and finally the fish begins to move back toward him. He takes the line up and soon the fish is there in the water just ten feet away. It is still deep and Jim cannot see him. He pulls him gently and soon the huge broad head comes into view. There they stop, the man looking at what is on the end of his line for the first time and the old fish seeing the first man he has seen for many years. There is enough time for Jim to gasp before the fish turns and once again makes a run for the pine. Again he is slowed before he can reach the tangle of sunken limbs and again Jim draws him close. This time when the fish turns there is panic and a touch of exhaustion and Jim feels it through the resilience of the bamboo. The fish makes two more runs before he begins to jump. He is huge but too tired to splatter the water with his tail and shake his head. Finally he lies in the shallows, listing to one side, and Jim pulls him gently over his net.

Then the fish is on the grass gasping for air and Jim sits beside him nearly as exhausted. He looks at the fish. He has never seen a fish like this before. He is as big as Jim's thigh in the center and three feet long. Looking back at the stream, Jim wonders how something like that could live in such a small body of water. He looks back to the bank and suddenly knows he can't take the fish away; he must *give him back.* Jim wants to take the fish home to show everyone, but he knows he can't. Then he remembers the hog-ring pliers in the old leather case on the side of the creel and he knows what he should do. Quickly he takes out the pliers and a ring. He fits the ring into the pliers so they are ready to close the ring tight on itself. He kneels beside the old fish and picks up the wide black tail. As he aligns the ring so that it will go into the gristly part of the tail, he notices something there in the tail, half an inch from the spot he has chosen to put the ring. With his free hand he touches it and scratches it with his thumbnail. It is a hog ring, old and nearly corroded through, forced through the gristly tail by the same pliers he is holding now. Jim looks to the head of the fish and stares, expecting him to be looking back. But he is gasping and Jim squeezes the pliers, quickly setting the new ring beside the old. Then he picks the old fish up and gently places him back in the pool. The fish lies there for a moment circulating the water through his gills. Then with an easy movement of the tail, he passes into the deeper water and is gone.

But he isn't really gone, Jim thinks.

And in the last light from the sun Jim makes his way back to the old ash tree. There he lays the creel down, disassembles the rod, and puts it into its battered case. He turns then and watches the sun flicker through the pines. It is still midafternoon in California, he thinks. It is probably hot and noisy. But here everything is silent except the stream. It rustles through his consciousness now. He closes his eyes and listens. When his eyes open again they are bright and in the twilight the stream is reflected within them. He leans over and picks up the old rod. He adjusts the creel strap on his shoulder and looks to the sun as it falls in a crash of color.

Weightless

Maggie told him a long time ago that there was nothing left between her and Mulholland. She said that Mulholland was in love with the mountain and nobody's marriage was big enough to include a mountain. It was years later that Mulholland had told him you could hear the earth's heartbeat if you held your ear to the North Face of the Grand Teton. That kind of talk was strange for Mulholland. He almost never talked about the mountain, and when he did it was not in metaphors. They had both been drinking that night and it had made sense to Cramer. But he never thought he would find himself pressing his ear tightly against the Grand's granite North Face and straining his senses to hear a sign of life.

Tonight he'd done many things he thought he'd never do. And so it seemed somehow natural, now, tied into pitons driven into the ledge, with light freezing drizzle coming down, to lean against the cold rock and listen for the earth's heartbeat. To hear it would be soothing, Cramer thought, like pressing his cheek against Maggie's shoulder in the night. His body went on with what it was doing and he let his mind float. He thought of Maggie and listened to the rock. Her face came to him, smiling, the face of fifteen years ago. The beginning rock-climbing class that he and Mulholland had taught. She liked climbers, she said. The better they were, the more she liked them. He could hear the laughter in her voice, but no matter how hard he concentrated he could hear nothing in the rock. All he could hear on the North Face of the Grand Teton was the clicking of the Maasdam winch he worked steadily with his right arm.

And he could feel the load: a young climber from Vermont, broken leg, lacerations, possible internal injuries, and shock. The litter came up, through the dark, inches at a time. It didn't catch on rocks or swing from side to side, because Mulholland was guiding it. He could feel Mulholland climbing smoothly beside the litter. Cramer knew that when Mulholland appeared at the ledge the litter would be tied to him, in case something happened at the winch. They'd been raising now for over four hours. When they made the ledge that Cramer was on they'd rest, if Mulholland agreed, then rope together and climb the next hundred and twenty feet to the Second Ledge, where Reynolds had talked about landing the helicopter. When they got there they'd secure the Maasdam winch again and Mulholland would go down and bring the boy up. Cramer had tried to talk Mulholland into trading off on the first two raises, but they both knew that Mulholland would be better at climbing up with the litter. Cramer had already decided that he wouldn't even offer to climb on the last raise. He knew that he was too tired.

Now he switched arms. He began working the handle of the winch with his left. This adjustment allowed him to move his body away from the face, and for an instant he thought he could see the glow of Jackson Hole below him. He knew that he was imagining the glow. He was much too high. There were thousands of feet of clouds between him and the city. But he let his imagination drift in the fog and in an instant he saw Maggie at the window of their house and he wondered if she'd figured out what was happening. His head floated, allowing him into his own exhausted daydream. She smiles at him and touches the curtain lightly with her left hand. "I know you're up there," she says. "I called Schmit when you didn't come home from the rescue meeting. He told me what Kevin said and I know that you are both on the mountain."

Cramer nods his head. "Don't worry," he whispers.

"But you know I will," she says. "I'll worry about the dark and the rain. I'll worry about you. I'll worry about Kevin."

The sound of Mulholland's jumars on the rock just below the ledge jumbled the daydream. For a moment Cramer's mind went blank, but he continued to work the winch. He shook his head, frightened now of dreaminess, trying to fight the fatigue and concentrate on what he was doing. He worked the winch steadily but more slowly, giving Mulholland more time to guide himself and the young climber over the lip.

When Mulholland's hand came over the edge Cramer stopped. He disconnected the carabiner and moved toward them. He switched on a small flashlight whose batteries he'd been trying to conserve. The light fell on the top of Mulholland's orange climbing helmet. The litter was behind and below him. He was not moving, still gathering his strength to come over the lip. When he turned his face toward Cramer it was dirty, strained, and streaked with sweat. He was clearly exhausted, clearly reaching down into the reserve of strength that always fascinated Cramer.

Cramer stood in the dark looking downward. Still disoriented, he thought of Mulholland, his climbing instinct, the graceful way he moved, his cool detachment from life. "There's no sense hating each other," Mulholland said, and Cramer shook his head knowing Mulholland was not speaking and that the words were from six years before. "You and Maggie are a natural," he said. "We might as well be civilized and sensible."

But now, standing wet and cold on the ledge above Mulholland, Cramer did not feel civilized. It was all he could do to resist the impulse to step on Mulholland's hands as he began to scramble onto the ledge.

"Give a pull on the rope, Ron," Mulholland said. "Gently."

Cramer took the rope in his hands and snapped himself back into the piton. He pulled Mulholland, and the boy came to a rest securely on the ledge.

"How's he doing?" asked Cramer.

"About the same," Mulholland said. "He ought to make it until morning."

"What if the weather stays shitty?"

Mulholland was breathing deeply, trying more to relax than to catch his breath, a trick to call up more endurance. "If Reynolds can't make it in by noon he'll go belly-up."

Cramer's flashlight swung to Mulholland's face. "We've got two hours until light."

"Hope they've figured out that their rescue is underway." Mulholland smiled in the flashlight beam. Behind him his shadow rolled twice life-size on the rocks of the cliff face. Cramer watched the shadows as Mulholland moved; the scene was eerie.

"Save the light, Ron." Mulholland touched Cramer's arm. "We may need it."

They tied the boy from Vermont into the ledge, under an overhang where the rain missed him and where any rocks that might kick loose would miss him too. They tied themselves together with a climbing rope and rechecked their equipment. Then they stood for an instant staring at each other in the dark. The rock above was vertical, loose from the rain. They knew that there was an easier way to the Second Ledge, but as Mulholland had said at the meeting, there wasn't enough time. The Vermont boy would be dead by midmorning, noon at the latest. The only way was straight up the face.

It had been a matter of time from the beginning. They'd both had their gear ready when the ranger station had called them. And though flying up was the obvious way, the weather had been too bad. No helicopter could fly until the next morning at best. So while the others argued over the details, they had jerked their gear from the backseats of their cars and set out walking in the rain. They'd made the Lower Saddle probably before they were even missed.

Mulholland had been standing near the back of the room, quiet as always, until Schmit had made the decision to wait for the weather to clear. When Mulholland heard that, he spoke. The others were speaking loudly, making plans for extra help, air support, and a supply line. Mulholland spoke softly, much lower than the others, but his voice prevailed. Everyone heard him say that if they waited for the weather to clear, they were really planning a body recovery and they could forget about a rescue. He pointed to the frightened partner of the Vermont boy. "You heard what he said—fractures, shock, in an exposed place. He's so much meat if we don't get up there right now."

Schmit's forehead and upper lip were sweating as he shook his head. "Christ, Kevin, look out that window. There's a fucking monsoon out there."

Mulholland didn't bother to look. "We could get to the Upper Saddle by dark if we started right now. We could do the contouring in a couple of hours and be on the North Ridge by eleven o'clock."

"I can't put anybody in jeopardy like that. The rescue waits for the weather."

Mulholland looked to Harry Reynolds, who leaned against another wall. "Can you land on the Second Ledge?"

Reynolds wore sunglasses and a flight jacket. He was Vietnam cool. "If the weather breaks," he said.

"Forget it," Schmit had said. "We wait for the weather and that's final."

The planning went on but when Cramer looked up a few minutes later Mulholland was gone. He knew that if he was going to catch up he'd have to leave the meeting quickly. He stood up and eased toward the door.

Now Cramer could only feel Mulholland in the dark. He felt the green eyes. "I'll go first," Cramer said.

Mulholland caught his arm and instinctively Cramer jerked it away. "I'll go first," Mulholland said. There was another moment of staring in the dark.

"Right," Cramer said. And Mulholland altered his stance.

He changed then, from a man in a helmet standing on a ledge to a climbing machine. Cramer felt him move away and upward. It was like being in the dark with a cat. The way Mulholland moved made Cramer wonder if the green eyes could see in the dark, if something in the mountain was guiding his hands and feet to the exact places where he would be safe.

The climbing was silent except for the occasional hollow ping of granite chips bouncing down the face. Now Cramer's fingers were cold from the rock and the dampness. Some of the crevices were still filled with ice. Even with numb fingertips, he could feel the velvet of the ferns and lichen entombed by the ice. He was usually slightly nervous when someone else was establishing his protection. He tried to be nervous now but could not do it. Now he was only cold— cold and exhausted.

Mulholland had found a good route to a small ledge, and were it not for the fatigue and the weight of the Maasdam winch on Cramer's back, the climb would have been easy. They stood again, inches apart in the darkness.

"I think the Pendulum Pitch is right over there," Mulholland said. He pointed into the darkness at their right. "The widest spot on the Second Ledge should be right above us, about eighty feet." Cramer nodded to himself. That meant they had come only forty feet.

"You ready, Ron?"

Cramer heard Mulholland but didn't answer. "You ready?"

"Yeah," Cramer said finally. "Let's go."

"This part has some of that lousy yellow rock," Mulholland said. "And it's icy."

"Right," Cramer said.

They started up, unprotected but roped together. The yellow rock was soft and crumbled beneath the toes of their boots. Cramer heard Mulholland swear softly in the darkness above him and shone his light upward.

"It's okay, Ron," Mulholland called down. "There's a tough spot up above me. Do you feel like a climb?"

Cramer looked over his shoulder. To his amazement the sky had begun to lighten. Now Maggie was in the kitchen. Cramer could see her pacing, sipping at the coffee. The hot coffee. And he could see that she hadn't even tried to sleep. "Terra firma," she said. "You've got both feet planted firmly on the ground." She'd told him. "That's what I like in a man," she'd said. Like, he thought. Not love. And he could see steam rising from her coffee cup.

"Do you feel like a climb?" Mulholland shouted. "There's a tough spot above me."

Cramer began to nod his head. Finally, as if the nodding had shaken it loose, he yelled, "I'm ready if you are."

The rough spot was a twisting chimney of the poor yellow rock. It was a forty-foot severe-pitch climb that would take them to the Second Ledge. Mulholland was on a tiny ledge six feet above Cramer's head.

"Belay me," Mulholland said as he checked to be sure he was tied in securely.

Cramer settled into a crevice and began feeding rope out as Mulholland started up. The rock was smooth and crumbly, and Cramer could imagine Mulholland falling. Mulholland was moving carefully and nearing the top, thirty feet above. He would fall sixty feet before the rope would go taut. Both men would receive a tremendous shock if he fell. Mulholland's life would be in Cramer's hands.

But Mulholland didn't fall. He climbed beautifully, extending himself to create pressure and friction where there were none. He arched his body in the growing dull light and pulled himself up with muscles that, in most men, had never developed. Sitting wedged in the rocks below, Cramer admired him. He felt silly belaying him. For Mulholland, gravity did not seem to exist.

Then he heard Mulholland call down that he was on the Second Ledge. It was Cramer's turn. Now it was Mulholland, secured above, who controlled the lifeline. Cramer was tired, disoriented. But he called up that he was beginning his climb.

When he reached for the first handhold a wave of vertigo swept over him. It frightened him and he pressed his face against the cold rock to stop it from spinning. He could hear Maggie telling him how much she hated the mountain. She was saying she was afraid of it. For the first time Cramer wondered if her hate was really jealousy.

The yellow rock of the North Face of the Grand felt gritty under his fingertips. It rolled like grains of sand under any pressure that he exerted. He told himself to lean out, away from the rock. He tried to climb with confidence. As Cramer entered the chimney he could feel the updraft. The air was changing. The weather would clear. He could feel a difference in the air pressure close to the rock. He could feel it in his ears.

The chimney where Mulholland had gone up was icy, and Cramer could see that the ledges to the left were bare and dry. He wondered why Mulholland had taken the chimney. He decided to climb out and go up the rock on the outside. The sun had shone more on the rock and somehow that seemed important. He slid sideways and pulled himself up. There were good handholds and he stood resting for a moment. When he looked up he could see where his belay rope disappeared over the rock. He was nearly to the Second Ledge. Only a small outcropping stood in his way.

The outcropping was darker granite, and as Cramer put his hands over the top of it and swung out he noticed that the rain had washed along the seam between the outcropping and the crumbly yellow rock of the chimney. He knew that he had made a mistake before he felt the outcropping shift, but there was no time to correct. The outcropping tore away from the mountain with a hollow cracking sound and everything began to fall in slow motion. Cramer had time to think about the climber from Vermont. He wondered if it had been like this for him. He thought about how mad Schmit would be. He thought of Maggie and he had time to tell her how much he loved her.

When the rope went taut it surprised him. He had forgotten there was a chance that Mulholland could hold him. He was surrounded by the sound of the avalanche and soaked in the pungent smell of exploding rocks. Somewhere above him he could feel Mulholland straining to hold on, trying desperately to cheat gravity.

He waited for the rope to give. He felt it stretch and saw Maggie clearly at the window. She held her hands up to him and he reached for her. By the time he realized that he was not going to die he was dangling, somewhere far above the earth, spinning slowly with his arms stretched out into space.

Only when he realized that Mulholland was secure did Cramer scream, long and mournfully, extending his fingertips and straining every muscle to touch the image of Maggie's outstretched hand.

He hung there for a long time, trying to think but finally giving up and letting his body react. He rolled into a sitting position and took his jumars from his climbing belt. He tied them into the belt and snapped them to the climbing rope. Slowly, on liquid arms and legs, he ascended.

When he got to the Second Ledge his face was white and his knees jerked in uncontrollable spasms. For a long time he didn't talk. He let Mulholland set the Maasdam winch and tie him into the rock.

"Reynolds is going to be able to fly. He'll be able to get at least the tips of his skids on this ledge," Mulholland said. "I'm going down for the kid. Can you work the winch?"

Cramer stared up at him. "Hell yes, I can work the winch," he said.

And so, while the eastern sky grew lighter, Cramer cranked the winch. He did not think. He simply pulled at the winch handle. When Mulholland and the litter came into view, Cramer went to help. Together they pulled the boy up and onto the broad, flat ledge.

"He's holding his own," Mulholland said. "If Reynolds can fly, this is going to work."

Cramer did not speak. They secured the litter. Reynolds' helicopter couldn't carry the boy, Cramer, and Mulholland, so they readied the ropes for one of them to descend to the First Ledge, the first step on the way back to the Upper Saddle.

And then they sat in silence, waiting, trying once again to rally strength. Mulholland closed his eyes when they first heard the popping of the helicopter blades. The helicopter was still far below them, but they moved to their feet. They stood side by side. Then Cramer turned to Mulholland.

"Why?" he said.

"Why what?"

"Why'd you stop me?" Cramer's teeth were clenched.

Mulholland was coiling a small piece of rope. He looked at Cramer from the corners of his eyes. "Don't be stupid, Ron," he said, and went to get the boy from Vermont ready to strap to the helicopter.

As the helicopter whipped closer Mulholland checked his equipment for the descent off the mountain. He coiled the ropes carefully and laid them where they would not be in the way of moving the litter. When the helicopter was very near Cramer came to him.

"You ride the chopper down," Cramer said.

"No," Mulholland said as he took a firm grip on one side of the litter. The wash from the rotor blades began to sweep the ledge. They knelt down and squinted their eyes. They could see Reynolds now, both hands steady on the controls, moving the helicopter very slowly toward the ledge. "You ride down!" Mulholland yelled.

The helicopter skids touched the edge of the ledge and they watched Reynolds' face for a sign. Almost imperceptibly Reynolds' head nodded. They raised the litter and moved into the skid closest to them. They strapped the litter in place.

"Get in!" Mulholland screamed.

"Why me?" Cramer shouted back.

They stared at each other for an instant and let the rotor wash pound them. "Because somebody's waiting for you!" Mulholland yelled. They glanced at Reynolds, gritting his teeth now, trying to hold the helicopter steady. Their eyes caught one more time, then Cramer scurried for the helicopter.

After the helicopter had pulled up and away from the ledge it pivoted slowly and hung there. From the helicopter door

Cramer could see Mulholland coming off the face. He flipped huge loops of his climbing rope out into space and fell in slow, flat arches. He bounced effortlessly from the cold granite as new loops snaked from his right hand. He touched the rock gently, plummeting earthward, caressing the North Face as he moved.

The Wild Geese

They had flown this way for nine springs now. The stops were always the same: the mountain lake, still locked with ice and nestled high in the Uintas, the flat corn stubble along the Platte River, and now the marshy prairie pond on the northern plains. From the croplands along the Platte to the prairie stopover was a short flight; easy with the extra energy from the days of full feeding on the corn left in the fields. The gander saw the pond, still miles off, and set his wings. He stretched them to full length. The span was diminished slightly on the left side from the lead shot lodged in the last joint of the wing. The dry prairie wind whistled in the primaries where they were permanently twisted.

He moved his broad head slowly from left to right and back again. His long, slender neck rotated and arched as he surveyed the flatlands below him. Except for the fresh plowing at the east end of the pond everything looked the same. He flared his wings to let the goose know that they would stop. When she came up next to him they began their bank into the wind. With their wings set and their tails spread slightly they began to descend. They dropped a hundred feet in seconds. The air screamed in their wings and the deck feathers of their tails vibrated in unison as they slowed, reversed their bank, and flattened out as if buoyed up by an invisible updraft. They glided over the pond at five hundred feet, the gander and the goose both watching for any sign of movement. It was a large pond and at one end a muskrat made his way across. Ripples grew in his wake until the pond's banks absorbed them. Redwing blackbirds were setting up territories in the reeds at the upper end. Their chattering came to the geese, who turned their heads to be sure of the sound. Now they were running downwind and gaining speed. When they came to the end of the pond they banked as one and hung, coming into the wind then, as if suspended from above. The upwind run was slower and they let themselves down halfway to the surface of the water. At the other end of the pond they turned for their last look before committing themselves to land. That was when the gander saw the man and woman. They walked along the bank and did not look up. Immediately the gander flapped his wings, the first flapping since the pond had come into sight, and the goose flapped her wings with him. But it was spring and this pond had never had hunters in the spring. They held their altitude and overflew the humans. The gander noticed that the muskrat paid them little mind. He swam slowly below them, pushing out more ripples, and the redwing blackbirds continued their contests in the reeds. The goose rotated her head toward the gander. He watched the humans and at the end of the pond again swung into the wind. The whistling in his left wing changed pitch as he forced the flat surfaces of every primary against the wind. They dropped almost vertically into a small secluded bay of the pond: as far from the humans as they could get.

The water of the pond felt prairie warm. It was barely spring on the prairie, cooler than the wintering ground of California and warmer than the nesting grounds would be. They could feel the winter lingering in the water, but the sun was hot and shone through cloudless skies. They could feel the promise of summer in the water. It was familiar, the same water they had settled into the spring of their second year. That was the first year they had made the migration together. But when they landed the gander did not hesitate. He swam to the point where he could look across the pond. He did not reveal himself but, by putting a portion of the bank between himself and where the humans were walking, he could raise his head and see that they had not seen them land, that they were intent on searching the bank at the other end of the pond. The gander could see that the man carried stones in his right hand.

The goose climbed onto the tiny island that they used each spring and fall when they passed through. They would sleep on the island for safety, conserving their strength for the long flight over the forests of North America that would start very early the next morning. Now the island was five feet in diameter and ten feet from the bank. But in the fall, when they returned with their brood in the good years, the water was smaller and the island bigger, the shore much closer. In the fall they could all sleep on the island, but often it was not far enough from the bank to keep the coyotes away. They had lost goslings at this pond.

The gander watched the humans for a long time. They kicked at the reeds along the bank but that was all, so he swam back to the island and climbed up to lie down beside the goose. She honked softly and preened the feathers of his long neck as he continued to watch, his head and neck extended periscopelike from the prairie grass. Finally she slept. She needed more rest than he; more strength, because she was growing the eggs inside her. The eggs must come within days of their arrival on the nesting grounds. If not, the early fall snows would lock them in with the goslings, cover the tundra, and take their grazing away. The goslings would die if they were not ready to fly south by the time the snow came. But some years it didn't matter. Some years there was no chance. Some years the snows covered the nesting grounds when they arrived. In those years the competition for nesting sites clear of the snow was fierce, and since there was no darkness on the nesting grounds the gander would fight day and night, protecting a small section of dry tundra where the goose could lay and incubate the eggs. He would be continually locked in battle with other ganders and do his best to keep other females, desperate to lay their eggs, away from the tuft of snowless grass that he had staked out for their nest. And there would be the ever-present arctic foxes, ready at any time to steal the eggs. He would fight them too, beat them with his wings, bite their necks and faces, fight them as if there were a chance of killing them. They would get some of the eggs but not all of them. By fall the gander would weigh only a portion of his present weight, but, with luck, there would be goslings to lead away from the nesting grounds.

And each year it got harder for him. The shot in the wing

had hampered him. He had received the crooked leg when the flat-faced human had caught them, flightless from the molt, leading the goslings across the tundra to good grazing. The club had come down hard and now it was difficult to keep his balance when he twisted an opponent's head down and into the tundra. It was possible that this would be his last migration, that they would fail this year, that he and the goose would have to join the outcasts at the edge of the nesting grounds, wandering and grazing where they could, honking pitifully toward where the strong birds raised the next generation of migrants. But that hadn't happened yet. Now, with the goose close beside him, her head tucked behind her wing, he was still the gander, watching every quadrant for movement, ready to sound an alarm or fight if he must.

But the prairie was peaceful in springtime. Occasionally he would let the warm, pure sunlight soak into him and he would doze. They passed the day that way, and as the sun began its descent into western cloud banks they began to feel restless. It would soon be time to swim to the bank and begin their evening grazing. The gander pushed off from the island first and again swam to where he could see the humans. They had pitched a tent but were again searching the banks, a stone in the man's hand. They were far away, but the gander saw the frog leap just as the stone exploded the water beside it. The sudden action alerted the gander, but the humans were a long way away and night was coming fast. The muskrat and redwing blackbirds had become active again. There was no danger for the present. The goose joined him in the water and together they swam in an elongated arc, drinking and dipping their heads under the water. They finally touched the bank and climbed up and out.

Now it was dark and they wandered through the marsh grasses along the bank until they came to the flat prairie. This was the first hard grass they had had since leaving the prairie the fall before on their way to the San Joaquin. The wheat-grass and bluestem were greening at their bases and were

sweet and tender. They meandered slowly through dry old
grass and wriggled their beaks down into this year's fresh
growth. They sheared the grass off and made chuckling noises
as they ate. In this way they passed the first part of the night.
The moon came up and shone down on them ghostly white.
Their shadows were cast black against the prairie grass.

And finally they were full. They could feel the soothing, sat-
isfied pressure in their crops and moved back to the pond and
slid into the water. Again they swam in an arc, this time in the
moonlight, and ended at the island. The muskrat purred past
them and they watched him together. And then they slept,
knowing that in a matter of hours they would begin again
their northward migration. By early afternoon they would be
over the pine forests of Canada that separated the prairie
from the tundra. There would be no stopping until the trees
began to dwarf and the muskeg appeared.

Their dreams were filled with endless horizons, airy vision,
and the silence of flight. The arctic foxes came in the dreams
and the goose woke twice when she heard the gander hissing
in his sleep. The moon had slid behind the Black Hills and the
prairie was dark. The wind scurried through the grass, and
the goose pressed against the gander and let her slender neck
drape across his back.

The first rays of sunlight found them like that: warm and
secure on their island and so close together that they were
almost one bird. The gander woke first. Something nagged at
his consciousness, a danger perhaps, and so he did not jerk
his head up but slowly opened his eyes. At first he did not see
the humans because they stood quietly, half-concealed in the
reeds on the bank ten feet away. But when the man knelt and
picked up a smooth stone, the gander's soul was buffeted as
surely as if it had flown into the drafts at the edge of a thun-
derstorm. Yet he did not let himself panic. He raised his head
slowly to face them, and the motion instantly woke the goose.
She did not move; she opened her eyes and felt the gander's
heart beating in her neck. She stayed perfectly still, knowing

that there was no time to get away, that there was no escape. She would depend on him. And so the gander, veteran of nine summers on the breeding grounds and nine seasons over the guns, raised his head and arched his thick neck. He stared into the eyes of the humans and let his eyes go black as the arctic sea. In those eyes were the cruelest of winds, subzero nights, days without food, and millions upon millions of wing-beats. He held them for a moment with the eyes, then, from his very center, he began to hiss. The sound was low-pitched and came from very deep inside the gander, the center of his wildness. An ancient sound, primordial, and something that the man and woman had never heard. It escaped on the gander's breath, changing pitch and intensity, the eyes blacker still and the wings flared. The hiss vibrated in the air. The grass trembled and the surface of the water shattered. The humans were afraid and their eyes widened like children's. It was as though they had stumbled upon a terrible secret. They drew back and the stone slipped from the man's hand. The gander held them for an instant more, but when the noise came again the humans recoiled and shrank back into the reeds. Still the geese did not move. The goose kept her head and neck pressed against the gander's back; her eyes were open and she gazed toward the open sky. The gander's neck remained arched and hard. He continued to focus his energy and his stare on the backs of the retreating humans.

They stayed that way until the sun was fully above the horizon. Then, without a sound, they rocked to their feet, slid into the water, and drank. Then slowly they paddled to the downwind side of their bay. The prairie breeze was fresh and they lifted from the water easily. They flew with the northwest wind quartering from their left and were two hundred feet above the tent when they passed over it. The breeze lifted them and gave them a lightness that allowed the gander to set his wings and survey the little camp while still gaining altitude. The air whistled in the feathers of his left wing and his eyes caught the stares of the man and woman once more.

But now the gander's eyes were placid. He watched the humans for a few seconds only, then looked away and set his
eyes on the northern horizon. The geese gained altitude as
they flew on. They became tiny dots, then faded completely
into the blue northwestern sky.

Strand of Wire

Framed in the square lines of the farmhouse window Judith Nelson watches her husband walk. She notices the limp yet she can still see the strength. She can see the power that was important so long ago. She stands with her head up, in front of the kitchen sink. Her husband walks toward the growing bean field. The morning sky is pink and brightening in front of him. His stiff black boots push up tiny billowing clouds from the dusty lane. They are like the giant afternoon clouds that rise black in the west. Judith's hand dangles absently into the cooling dishwater. Two plates are beside the sink, the breakfast untouched, cold.

There is a numbness. Since Billy Knutson died she has known this morning would come, but she has never understood. She has listened to her husband, never saying what he meant but telling her just the same. Telling her he was afraid. Wishing he had the money to buy the Knutson place, wondering who would have it. And worry, a terrible worry about the fence and the people who would own its other side. There would be that awful awkwardness.

The fence had belonged to the two of them, Billy Knutson and her husband; they had mended it together. Now it would be according to the law. *Face the fence, standing on your land. The half of the fence to your right is your responsibility.* There would be strangers there. Not like before. Not the Knutsons, or the Olsens, or the Johnsons. They were all gone, dead, moved, gone away. Of the old times only the river remained. And she thinks of the river, there even before her parents, constant, chewing quietly at their back pasture.

Except for the oldness, the slowness, the walk is the same. She has known it since she was a child. He leans forward, into the walk, swinging the left hand, jerking it up almost to his chest. It is the way he used to run. The same as sixty years before, wide-eyed, speaking a different language, running to the schoolhouse, running to bring the cow, running to their own church, gone now. And thinking back she can see that even then the signs were there. This morning had been coming since then.

Billy Knutson had been the last. He would visit them, drink coffee and talk to her husband of horses that wore size ten shoes and plowed without a line. They would laugh sometimes and the sound would be funny, like from a dream. And sometimes they would drink whiskey and speak, then, the old language and they would talk about the disappointments, shake their heads at their parents' choice of land, wonder at the ocean whose memory forced their parents to settle beside the river. The wild, fouled, fishless river that moved, not by tides but by the twisting power of the land itself.

And that talk would make them silent. They would grip each other's forearms and shoulders. But Billy Knutson was gone. Five years now. And his farm was owned by a man they did not know. Only that he was from the east, that he had new tractors and a combine that harvested six rows at a time and that he squeezed the land for all it was worth. She did not know him to see him but she could feel him all around them. Except for the narrow right-of-way Billy had insisted that her husband accept, they had no access to the road. They were captive there, between the river and the rusting wire fence that they shared, now, with a stranger.

Their farm had been diminishing since before she could remember. Every spring the river would claim another section of crumbling bank, and even in dusty August handfuls of topsoil washed daily into its rolling belly. Judith had watched him walking the riverbank, gazing across its width. Walking the boundaries of his land and stopping to stare at a spot in the river, remembering when he had stood there and gazed even further out to where the river boiled brown, almost thick. Then he would look up stiffly and go on. Until he came to where the river turned and where the boundary fence began, appearing rusty, ghostlike, from the water. And he would turn and walk that boundary for two miles. Along the way he would pull up the sagging wires, twist the broken ends back

together, make the fence stand if he could. But along its entire length, from where it appeared to where it descended
again into the river, he knew that hungry cattle would be
pushing at it from the other side, straining at his corn and
beans and that, as always, it would give to their weight. And
once, though he never said he had, she knew that somehow
he had made himself go to the neighbor's house, according to
the law, and asked to share the cost and labor of a new fence.
She knew this because she had seen him return, sit in the
pickup after the engine died, then slowly open the door,
swing his feet to the graveled drive, and show her his chalk-
rock face, dusted with years of disappointment and now the
courage spent.

So it had been five years that he had raised a crop to feed to
the neighbor's cattle, and each year the land growing smaller
and the price of the crops he could glean from the fields getting lower and lower. Until she had told him that something
must be done. She had never meant it to come out the way it
did, it had come out hard and cold and when it was out he
stared up at her from the table. His gray eyes were steady into
hers and for an instant she thought that she had been wrong,
that there was no trouble in his world. But she had been
right, the eyes narrowed and he was forced to look away.

She lets some water out of the sink and warms what is left
with hot from the spigot. Her husband is further down the
lane, still sending up dust from around his feet, walking with
his limp past the grown-up weeds of their grove. And hiding
in those weeds is the story of the farm. Obscured from sight,
laid in rows surrounded by waist-high weeds, are the rusted
walking plows, the rotted harness, and the discarded corn
knives. One row closer are the steel seats and boilers of the
days of steam, and closest to where her husband is walking
are the one- and two-row cultivators and plows. And gasoline
engines from tiny tractors that stopped running years before.
Even now she knows that in the machine shed there is nothing
that can turn the ground, plant the seed, or harvest the crops

more than three rows at a time. That, she decides, is part of the trouble. But a small part. The rest of the trouble goes deeper than even steel can penetrate. It has to do with flesh, with something inside that man walking away and with something that will die with him, would have died with Billy Knutson but didn't. It crawled from the cheap wooden casket that day in November and into her husband's chest. And when he stood up from where he'd sat alone all night he carried the trouble that Billy had gathered from this land, inherited from the others. Her husband was silent then, frightened and crippled by the burden.

Almost a year ago he brought home enough material to fix his share of the fence. Borrowed the money, she imagined, and unloaded the fifteen spools of wire and the bundles of fence posts beside the barn. The next morning he walked out to begin fixing his half of the fence. He walked the same direction that he is walking now but in a different way. He had made many trips, carried the posts and wire, struggled with them, and she had seen that the loads were too much for him. But last year she had been able to look down at the dishwater. This morning his load was lighter. The wooden butt of his rifle slapped against his lame leg with every step, and for the second time she notices that the water is going cold.

He had fixed his share of the fence, from the river to the center of the boundary. He worked alone, for three weeks, steady. When it was finished he waited for the spring which came that year, as always, overdue yet catching everyone unprepared. And when he went to the fields the neighbor's fence was still rusty, tumbled down. He said nothing. He plowed his land and planted it and watched his crops grow up as fast as the neighbor's pasture was grazed down.

He would stand at the end of the lane where he is standing now, watch across the field to where the cattle strained at the fence, stretching their bulky heads over and reaching for the pollinating bean plants. In the last days of September when it seemed the fence could hold them no more, he would wake up before light, stand in the kitchen, and stare into the darkness. Finally he would walk out to meet the morning and chase the cattle away from the fence, save his crops for another day.

And yesterday he stood out where he is standing now, watching the dusty pasture on the other side of the fence that could not feed the cattle for one day more. By morning they would be grazing in his beans as they had done every year since Billy Knutson died. And so that night the rifle came out from behind the door and at the kitchen table he sat wiping the barrel and sliding the oiled bolt in and out. But it was not the rifle that troubled Judith. It was the silence. All that evening and early, hours before sunrise this morning, there was silence. Not that it was different, there were never many words, but this morning in the darkened kitchen the old times lay thick on the counter and oozed out from around the cupboard doors.

When she awoke he was back at the kitchen table and she could hear that he was talking, a conversation. But when she came into the kitchen he was silent. And the bacon sizzled in the pan, moved to the table, and grew cast-iron cold on the plates in front of them. There were no words. Just the pale, brightening kitchen walls and her husband, slumped forward, pushing at the bacon with his fork.

When there was light enough to see he took the rifle from the corner where he had left it shining clean and slowly pushed shells into the magazine. They made a scraping sound, and Judith brought the dishes to where they are stacked now, beside the sink below the white-framed window. And from that window she watches the rifle come up to her husband's shoulder, sees the first puff of smoke, and the bellow and the crack from the rifle reach her ears at the same time. She feels frightened, helpless, and yet she holds her head up watching and listening to the deaths of the second and third cows and suddenly she knows what her husband has known since the beginning. She knows the coolness of his gray eyes, the steadiness of his hand in the half-light, sliding the cartridges into the rifle. She too is standing at the end of the lane, and she realizes what he would have said, had he spoken at all.

Final Touches

Peter and Marvin sat at the table in Peter's kitchen drinking coffee. It was Tuesday morning, the day before Peter was supposed to leave for California. Marvin wore an oily baseball cap pulled low, shading his dark eyes and stubbly cheeks. There was nothing on the table but a flowered china sugar bowl. Diane had not taken it when she left because the lid was broken. Once in a while, as they talked and drank their coffee, one of them would glance into the otherwise bare living room at the shiny black studio grand piano and comment on how heavy it looked.

Peter had a little headache. He had had a headache almost every Tuesday morning since Marvin got arrested for DWI. In addition to the week in the county jail, Marvin had been directed to go to AA meetings on Monday nights. It was part of his sentence. He had to go, but he wasn't allowed to drive. His license had been suspended, and Peter had to pick him up and drive him into town and wait while Marvin went to the AA meeting. There was no place to wait in Vermillion except the Charcoal Lounge. So while Marvin listened to testimonials from old winos about the pitfalls of alcohol, Peter drank draft beers and chased them with peppermint schnapps.

In return Marvin helped Peter when he needed it. Today Peter needed help packing and loading the piano into the pickup.

"I wish I was still in jail," Marvin said.

"Why?"

"So I wouldn't have to help you move that piano." He glanced into the living room.

"It won't be that bad," Peter said.

"Don't bullshit me. I helped you unpack it. I know how bad it's going to be."

"You were drunk that day."

"So were you."

"It'll be easier sober."

"Nothing's easier sober."

"More coffee?"

Marvin nodded and held his cup out. "How's she doing?"

"Who?"

"Come on."

"She sounds all right on the phone. She's got friends out there," Peter said. He wanted to tell Marvin that Diane was living with someone already, but he couldn't. "She's got friends in California."

"Friends?"

"A doctor that we used to know in Sioux Falls."

Marvin nodded. "Say," he said, "you got a little something to hop this up a bit?" He held up the coffee cup and smiled an innocent, missing-tooth smile.

"I thought you were supposed to lay off that stuff."

"Just when I'm driving. One more DWI and it's the state slammer. But I ain't driving." He squinted at Peter. "You could use a shot yourself."

Peter took the bottle of Windsor from the cupboard. He broke the seal and poured a shot or so into each cup. He felt a pang of embarrassment, a touch of remorse. He never thought he'd find himself drinking before noon. The time they'd unpacked the piano had been different. It had been the middle of the afternoon and very hot. Besides, Diane had drunk the beer with them, a kind of celebration for the new piano. He'd been hung over for days, hadn't had another drink for a month. But a lot had changed in the last five years. He looked at the brown liquid in the bottom of his cup. Marvin was watching him but Peter didn't drink.

"I didn't ask when you picked me up because I didn't want to know, but is that piece of junk in the back of your pickup the crate for the piano?"

"Yep."

Marvin drank.

It was December and the South Dakota countryside looked cold. There had been snow several times in the last few weeks. There was still an inch or so on the ground where the wind couldn't get at it. Peter could see the mailbox out the front window, its silverness gone gray in the light. He thought about the letter from Diane. She'd said it was eighty-two degrees. She'd said there was a palm tree in their yard and that oranges and tangerines grew in the backyard. Peter had trouble imagining oranges on trees. Impersonating apples, he thought. Orange trees in Diane's backyard; it was hard to believe, especially when Peter looked out the window and saw the bare oaks and ash trees around the house and the pasture. Diane had loved those trees, or said that she did. Now he was planning a trip to take what was left of her to California.

It had been part of the divorce; she got the piano. It made sense. What could Peter do with a piano? He could listen to someone else play it, and he could help move it. So that part seemed right. What troubled him was the part that left the delivery of the piano—an assumption, really—up to him. He didn't want to go to California. He didn't want to see Doctor Price again. He wasn't sure he wanted to see Diane again. But he had agreed to deliver the piano when she got settled. Well, the letter said that she was settled so he should bring it out. Just like that, as if it was fifty miles, or across town. Probably she didn't realize how far South Dakota was from California. Maybe she didn't know that the Rocky Mountains were in the way. Marvin had finished off his coffee and set the cup down on the table. "More?" Peter asked.

Marvin nodded and Peter filled the cup halfway, topping it off with Windsor. "Ain't you drinking?" Marvin asked, pointing to Peter's cup. Peter shook his head. "Not yet." They moved into the living room and sat on the floor. They watched the piano, pretending to be thinking about how they were going to attack it. They could hear the wind outside, could feel the dampness and the cold.

In a few minutes Marvin asked if Peter had a crescent wrench. Peter said he did. A while later Peter said that he had borrowed a dolly from Bob Cramer at the furniture store. Marvin said that would help.

Then, finally, as if a silent order had been given, they both rose to their feet. "Suppose we ought to bring the fucking crate in first," Marvin said.

The house faced south, and when they stepped out onto the porch that Peter had built he remembered the nights Diane and he had slept out there wrapped warm in the zip-together sleeping bags and watched the constellations. Orion was always his favorite. Sometime before midnight on early winter nights he used to appear in the sky to the south. He had always been easy for Peter to find. He could remember pointing him out to Diane, stretching his naked arm out into the cold air with Diane sighting along it from where she snuggled her head against his shoulder. Their breath had frozen as they whispered to each other. It had been a long time since he'd looked for Orion, a couple of years at least.

They stood on the porch and finished off their coffee. Then they stepped down and across the yard to the pickup truck. Peter hopped up into the bed and pushed the crate toward Marvin. It was an old crate he'd picked up in Vermillion at the furniture store. It had been in the back for years. "Been that long since I sold a real grand piano," Cramer had said. The wood was broken in several places and nails stuck out at odd angles. Marvin moaned when the weight shifted from the pickup to him. Peter jumped down and slid his end to where he could get a grip on it. The crate wasn't heavy but it was awkward. The wind buffeted it slightly as they made their way to the front door. When they got it inside they set it down gently. "Time for more coffee. More Windsor," Marvin said. He filled his cup and handed Peter's to him.

They sat down again and looked at the crate alongside the piano. "What d'you suppose it weighs?" Marvin said.

"Six hundred," said Peter.

"At least."

Marvin mused on the weight of the piano. "That'd be over twelve sacks of hog feed." A second later, "Three engine blocks. Two 700-80 tractor tires. Christ." He sipped and thought. "Maybe we could move it in pieces."

"The legs come off."

"Big deal."

Again they rose, pulled the piano out away from the wall, and walked around it. "We take a leg off first and set that side down on the floor," Peter said.

"Left foreleg or single rear?"

"Left fore, I figure."

"Then single rear."

"Yeah, and the right foreleg last. Then it's flat on the floor," Peter said. "We slide the crate around right beside it and tip the whole thing up and in."

"Simple," Marvin said, "if we had six guys to help." He walked around the piano one more time. "Better take them pedals off first," he said and pointed, "or Diane won't have nothing for her feet to do."

Peter took the pedals off and loosened the first leg while Marvin refilled their cups. This time he skipped the coffee. "Take ahold of this corner," Peter said; "I'm going to take the leg off."

"Oh sure, you think I'm going to hold the corner of that thing all by myself?"

"Just until I get the leg off and can get up to help you lower it."

"Jesus." Marvin put the cups down and braced himself at the corner of the piano. "Make it snappy," he said.

Peter knocked the leg out of the socket where it had been bolted and for an instant Marvin held the piano corner alone. "Hurry! Jesus! Hurry! Ahhh, whew!" And they lowered it to the floor together.

They sipped at their Windsors and studied the tilted piano. "Diane said to have it moved professionally."

"Now you tell me."

"Two hundred bucks just to drive down from Sioux Falls, crate it up, and load it into the pickup."

"You're going to owe me a hundred when this is over. Two hundred counting when we brought it in."

"The freight people put it on the porch for us, remember?"

"Hundred and fifty."

"Forget it."

The next two legs were easier, and in no time the piano was flat on the floor. It looked as though the legs had crashed through the floor. Now they moved the crate up along the straight side of the piano. "And we just tip it up and in," Peter said.

"Going to need some padding," Marvin said.

Peter looked. Of course; he remembered the foam rubber that had come with it. He sipped on his drink and thought. "Blankets, stuff like that," Marvin said. There wasn't much left in the house. Diane had taken most of it. Not that she'd stolen it; it was hers. Peter really didn't have a use for more than one blanket. There were a few burlap sacks in the barn, they could use them. And in the basement, sure, Diane had missed the sleeping bags.

"There are sacks in the tack room," Peter said. "I'll get an old sleeping bag from the basement."

There were a few spiderwebs on the stairway. Water had leaked in from the last fall storm. When they moved in, there had been no concrete floor. The house had been abandoned in the middle of renovation, two years before they bought it. The basement had been dug but they had never gotten around to pouring the floor. Peter had done it himself. That was before he'd met Marvin, before they'd met anyone, really. They'd just driven out from Ohio, seen this place, liked it, put all their savings down on it, and moved in. He remembered spending most of the night on his hands and knees troweling the cement, with Diane sitting on the basement steps helping where she could, bringing him snacks, and talking about how great it was going to be. Before they put the floor in the basement it had a smell like something Peter had never smelled before—decay, moisture trapped in the earth with no chance of escape. It had been perfect habitat for salamanders. That had been a big reason they'd been able to afford the place. Nobody wanted to live above a salamander den.

But now it smelled like a basement. His basement. Their basement. The salamanders were gone. There were rough shelves along one wall where the sleeping bags were. They'd bought them together, made them from kits, really, left-hand zipper for him, right-hand for her. The bags had always been kept together in one sack. He'd keep the sack, he thought. But by rights one of the sleeping bags was hers. Finding it protecting the piano would be a nice surprise for her.

He brought both bags upstairs and found that Marvin was into the Windsor again. Peter glanced at the clock on the stove. It was almost two o'clock. They stuffed the crate with feed sacks and Diane's sleeping bag. They lined it up perfectly so that the piano would tip right into it. Then they moved to the other side of the piano, hiked their pants up, took deep breaths, and squared their stances. They bent down and Peter counted backward from five. To their amazement it worked. The piano went right in. Peter went for the crate lid and a hammer while Marvin, still skeptical, kept one hand against the piano and slurped his Windsor with the other. They slipped the legs into the corner of the crate and nailed the lid in place. Then they sat down on the floor, leaning against the crate lid as if there were a tiger inside.

"A-fuckin'-mazing," Marvin said.

"A breeze."

"Now all we got to do is get it into the truck."

They strapped the crate to the dolly and rolled it easily out the front door. The sky showed signs of clearing but was still gray. There were three front steps and it seemed that the only way to get the piano down was for one person to push from the rear while the other lowered the front gradually. "I'll push," Marvin said.

They eased it down the first step and the center of the crate hung up. "Push hard," Peter said.

"You sure?"

"Push."

Marvin pushed and the front of the crate came off the next two steps, banged against the sidewalk, swayed as if it might tip over, and finally lodged halfway to ground level. For a moment it seemed certain that the piano would go over. "I wish I was still in jail," Marvin said.

"We're okay, the dolly just slipped. Come around and help me get it back on."

They lifted together and the dolly went back on. Then, more slowly this time, they moved the rear of the crate onto the sidewalk. They smiled at each other and wheeled it out to the pickup. The tailgate was down and hit the piano crate about midway up.

"Jesus," Marvin said. "Six hundred pounds four feet straight up."

"We need a jack or a ramp or something."

"We need a drink," Marvin said.

The bottle was half-gone.

"If we were at my place we could use my winch."

"But I don't have a winch."

"How about a tractor with a loader?"

"I'd have to borrow one from a neighbor. Besides, if we dropped it . . ." Peter winced at the thought.

"We'll never push it up a ramp. Like BBs up a rat's ass."

Peter agreed. "Probably break a two-by-ten. We'll have to use a jack."

"We'll be crushed," Marvin said, nearly to himself. He splashed more whiskey into his cup and reached over to fill Peter's.

"There are some cement blocks out by the shed. If we leave the dolly on, jack one end up, and back the pickup under it, then we can jack the other end up and block it. When it's level we just back the pickup the rest of the way and she rolls right in."

"We'll be crushed," Marvin said again. "They won't find us till the county man comes to plow the road."

The jack sank into the soft driveway but only a few inches. When the piano started up it went fast. Marvin steadied it, throwing blocks up as they went as a precaution against its slipping off the jack. By the time the edge of the crate looked high enough to get the pickup under it, the jack had nearly worked its way out from under the lip where Peter had hooked it. "Get in and back her up," Peter said, "quick."

The tailgate slipped under the tilted edge of the crate with little to spare. "I'm going to let her down," Peter said. "You ready?"

"Jesus, Jesus." Marvin put both hands on the crate. "Slow, now," he said.

When Peter began to lower the jack it slipped and the crate fell onto the tailgate. It fell only two inches but the pickup sagged and a faint, sick chord sounded from within. Marvin didn't break and run. He stayed right there and steadied it. "Jesus, Jesus." And the piano crate did not fall; it stood solidly, just as they had planned, with one end firmly on the ground and the other on the tailgate of the pickup.

They raised the rear of the crate very carefully, blocking it with every crank of the jack. Finally it was suspended three and a half feet off the ground, the front on the tailgate of the pickup and the rear on a stack of cement blocks. It loomed against the afternoon sky, the top eight feet off the ground. Now it was a matter of one of them holding the piano in place while the other slowly backed the pickup. The plan was for it to roll right in, but it seemed too high off the ground to Peter, too wobbly, too much chance for an accident. Now he was afraid. What if it tipped and fell? It would be smashed, totally ruined. He imagined the sound it would make as it hit the ground. What would Diane say? Would she think that he'd done it on purpose? Subconsciously?

But now it was too late.

"Who's holding and who's driving?"

Peter shrugged.

"It's Diane's piano," Marvin said. "If it's going to crush somebody seems like it ought to be you."

Peter nodded. "Okay," he said.

When Marvin started the pickup the piano trembled. The crate was just thin enough for him to put an outstretched arm and hand on each side and press his chest and cheek against the rear. He braced himself and closed his eyes as Marvin started back. He could feel some pressure and could hear the dolly wheels begin to roll along the bed of the pickup. When the tailgate knocked the pile of cement blocks down Peter grasped at the crate desperately, but the piano was already loaded. He felt Marvin turn the engine off and saw him get out, slam the door, and head for the house.

He was back in seconds with the bottle. "Un-fuckin'-believable," he said.

They drank the whiskey while Peter tied the piano into the pickup. Peter wasn't sure how it had happened but he was giddy now and getting drunk. He lashed the piano in tight. He tied half-hitches between sips of whiskey. Marvin didn't help. He walked around the pickup, holding the bottle by the neck and shaking his head. He held the bottle up and they toasted each other. "When you pull up out there in California with this rig, that doctor is going to have about twenty-five of his friends lined up to help unload it," he said. "They're going to look up at that fucking whale and say, 'Why, Peter, however did you get it up there?'" He laughed and drank from the bottle. "Tell 'em your old pal Marvin helped."

They sat on the porch as the sun went down. They watched the piano and finished the bottle of Windsor. It was getting very cold. Peter sat leaning against the railing along the steps. "It'll be a long trip," he said. "Might take me a week." He could see the evening star now. "Look there," he said, pointing. "Going to be clear and cold tonight." He turned but Marvin was gone.

When he went into the house he found Marvin asleep on the floor where the piano had been. The sleeping bag was still where he'd left it. He took it from the sack and went back outside. He climbed up into the pickup bed and laid his sleeping bag out on top of the piano crate. The bag was cold against his skin and the crate not very wide. He lay quietly on his back with his head turned toward the south. He thought that his mind would be full, but nothing came. He would wait, he thought, until Orion swung up from the southern sky and the stars began to sparkle and do their dance in the cold December night.

The Georgia Breeze

From this rocking chair I can see the whole place. My house is on the highest ridge in the country and beneath me I can see everything that ever meant anything to me. The ridge that I'm on is hardwood and rolls down to the dairy pastures where the gray-brown cows with black eyes stand chewing, staring into the thickets at the edge of the pasture like there might be something in there. And past them are the five- and ten-acre patches of corn and cotton, all of them connected by horse paths and ringed with brush. I can see the buildings and the house, probably two miles off, as much a part of what I see as the trees, or the grass, or the red clay that's under it all.

Sometimes I sit here and dream. And if I sit long enough, I can see the Georgia Breeze again, casting out around those field edges, running downwind of the fence lines, holding his head high. He's reading this place like it's all painted in black and white. I can see him glancing back over his shoulder, staying out in front, and sometimes I can see him swing into the wind and freeze, as if that instant God had turned him to stone. But mostly when I see him I see him running, long and smooth, covering the ground, running. Running like nothing else matters.

Like nothing else mattered. Like that was all that mattered. All that mattered to Mr. Morgan, frail and gray. Moving slowly now, down the steps of the house that has been in his family since before the Civil War. Waving away the women who try to help him. Walking with a cane to shake the hands of the men who have worked for him since they were boys. Old and sick, but the brightness still there, sunken in wrinkled sockets. He nods to each man. Then he comes to me, but not taking my hand, just reaching out and touching me and I follow him away from the rest and we walk the same way we've walked a thousand times. Through the break in the hedge and out to the kennels. And together we walk down the concrete path past each run and the pointers paw and force their noses through the wire at us.

Mr. Morgan touches them all, all except the big old brown-ticked pointer in the last run. When we get to him we stop. Mr. Morgan tells me, Jessie, the Morgan plantation is quite a place. I don't say a word, and he says, We got us a herd of registered dairy cattle, a lumber mill, a gin of our own, and some of the best crops in the state. I'm standing there nodding, not looking up, and he says, But the best thing is right here. We both look down the line at the dogs. Straight legs, loose skins, shiny eyes, and high, cracking tails. Without saying it we are both thinking back to the mountain curs that Mr. Morgan bred them from. Then he puts his thin hands through the wire of the last run and holds the old pointer's big square head and says, Take care of the Georgia Breeze, Jessie. He's the best pointer that ever pointed a quail, he says.

The best you got, he says. Go get the best you got, and I drop the manure fork and I'm back before he has time to bring them big walking horses out of the barn. Wonderful day, scent's just right, he says. And he smiles as he swings up into the saddle. And I think, Lord God, if I could only ride like that. Sitting tall, back straight as a fence post, glued to that little flat saddle like it's part of him. And the horse, sliding those feet out like he's glad to be doing it.

Mr. Morgan says, Let's try the new bitch and Sam. So I unsnap their leads and they're gone. The two other dogs that I brought out jump and tug at their lead ropes wanting to go with them. But once I'm in the saddle they quiet to a steady strain on the ropes and we head out, riding side by side, me holding the second pair of dogs and Mr. Morgan singing to the brace that's down so they know where we are and can stay out in front.

Sometimes I watch him, if I'm not watching one of the dogs, and I can tell when one comes into sight and I can tell if it's running like he likes to see them run. By Mr. Morgan's eyes or mouth I can tell if that dog is keeping its head and tail high. Like now, I can tell that the young white bitch is casting out, running the edge of the beans and I can tell that she's running good. I can see in Mr. Morgan's face that he's happy

with her. I knew it was a test 'cause he put her down with
Sam. He wants to know what she's made of. And by watching
his eyes, even from the side, I know an instant before he takes
his hat off and holds it high and shouts, Point, that she's found
a covey and I lean forward and let that walking horse rock me
across the bean field, flat out, the mud from Mr. Morgan's
horse splattering us and the wind ripping at my clothes.

We're getting closer and I can see that the bitch is on an
incline, her head lower than her rear and her whole body
curved. She's pointing a covey that's beside her, hiding twenty
feet away in the brush of the bean field edge. The dogs on the
leads stiffen up when they see her and refuse to take another
step. Mr. Morgan smiles as we dismount and before he takes
the shotgun from the saddle he strokes the two dogs who
have honored the bitch's point. I look to where the quail
should be and deep in the thicket I see another patch of white.
It's Sam, pointing the same covey from the brush. Mr. Morgan, I
say, and nod toward where Sam stands motionless. They got
them quail plumb bottled up, I say. Mr. Morgan nods and steps
up beside the white bitch, who has moved nothing, not even
an eyelid. He strokes her along the back and steps forward
into the covey.

The birds erupt, twisting and turning between the trees
and the shrubs, the sound of a hundred horses snorting, and
Mr. Morgan fires the shotgun into the air, not even watching
the quail but keeping an eye on each dog. They are both
stock still, only raising their heads slightly to see where the
quail are going. I tie the second pair of dogs and now I'm in
snapping a lead onto the little bitch and Mr. Morgan goes into
the thicket to bring Sam out.

He hands Sam's lead to me and steps back to look at the
two dogs. He's always trying to come up with something better and I know what he's thinking. He's thinking she's strong,
thinking that it's the mixture of blood that counts. Thinking
about blood. Blooded dogs, blooded horses, even people.

New people. New blood for the plantation. A new boss.

Mr. John Landeen, walking down the scrubbed bricks between the thick oak stalls asking me what Mr. Morgan had
kept the saddle horses for. For running the dogs, I tell him,
and he looks at me and smiles. For running dogs? he asks. He
swings his hand around the barn and ends up at the glass-
windowed tack room, the brass-fitted harness and the pol-
ished saddles. It's a museum, he says, and looks at me and
makes me feel old. There's just no place for it now, he says.
And I'm knowing he'll be sorry come quail season and I'm
wondering how I'll get them dogs ready without a horse. But
I say, Yes sir, to what he says and, Yes sir, to doing the kitchen
chores. And, Yes sir, to will a tractor fit in the barn, and, Yes
sir, yes sir.

Yes sir. I know what happens this Thursday. I heard it from
one of the girls in the house. Thursday you got people coming from town to go quail hunting, I say. Mr. Morgan nods at
me and I tell him, Yes sir, I know what that means. That means
them dogs best be looking good, and Mr. Morgan smiles.

And come Thursday those dogs are looking good. I'm out
front scouting up the dogs and Mr. Morgan is riding with his
guests and they're talking and Mr. Morgan is singing to the
dogs and they're putting on a show. They're everywhere and
finding more quail than there could ever be out in those
patches and I'm scouting them up, finding them pointing in
places they just couldn't be. I'm finding them dogs where
they might have never been found, and once in a while I
catch one lollygagging around behind the hunters and I quick
make him heel behind the horse and we scoot up through the
woods to where I can send him out in front and the people
don't ever know the truth and they think that dog has been
running out there where he belongs all along. Today I know
I'm earning my keep.

I'm scouting up a storm and it's all different. I'm right out
here with the dogs. I'm thinking like a dog. I'm figuring where
those quail are going to be and I'm making up my mind just
like a dog, where to go after I cast through that patch of

beggar-lice. And I'm always keeping in mind that no dog ever smelled a quail by running upwind of it. And I'm knowing that those dogs know all of that, better than me, and I got to think fast to keep up with them and I can't see the eyes so I can't tell what is happening like I can when I'm riding with Mr. Morgan so I stay one step behind. It's all different out here in the brush. Everything is faster.

Even the singing sounds different. From out here it sounds like it must sound to the dogs. It's distant, a kind of whining language that tells you where you are and means, if you can hear it at all, that everything is still all right.

And later they are all in the kennel talking about what a good hunt they had and what good dogs they are and I'm feeding the dogs and, when I open the last pen, five fat wiggling pointer pups tumble out onto the ground and one of the men says to Mr. Morgan, They're wonderful, and picks one up. The man picks them all up, one by one, and finally he says, Could I buy one. And Mr. Morgan says, No, but I'll give you one. Then he leans over and picks up a male pup that is sitting by itself. Anyone but this one, Mr. Morgan says, anyone but this one.

Anyone at all. Take them all if you want, anyone at all. And he swings that arm again, right down the line. These kennels are going, he says. The man says, Thank you, Mr. Landeen, and I just got to say, Mr. Landeen, I got two of them ready for you to go hunting and that old dog on the end ain't no good to nobody. Mr. Landeen says, The kennels have to go, Jessie. And I remind him that his boy wanted to go quail hunting. He'll be home from college any day, I say, and Mr. Landeen says, Okay, anyone but those three, and the man thanks him and right away I start working them two dogs like they ain't never been worked so when the day comes I am ready.

Ready for Thomas Landeen and his young friend to take them out quail hunting. But they get drunk, imagine that, drunk with guns and the dogs are right. They're running right, sucking up the ground and nobody watching but me. Mr.

Tom and his friend don't want to walk and they get the pickup stuck and I know them dogs are piled up somewhere on point waiting for us and we never get there and all I get is, Where are them damn dogs of yours, Jessie?

And after that, when I'm putting the dogs up them boys are drinking more on the porch and pretty soon I hear a shot and come on the run. I stop right beside the Georgia Breeze, who's watching to see about the shooting. I see them two boys walking down the steps of the house laughing and they look into a bush just off the lawn and they wave to me to come. And when I do, Thomas says, Jessie, this here is what we was looking for this afternoon. And he hands me a quail that he shot. That's what they look like, Jessie. And all I can say is, You shot it on the ground. That chasing dogs is crazy, Jessie. That little bastard was almost in the yard. Another minute and it would have run over there and bit that sorry old hound of yours. He points at the Georgia Breeze and they laugh. But the Georgia Breeze pays no attention. He yawns, lays stiffly down, and stretches out in the afternoon sun.

Stretches out. Look at him stretching out, taking in an acre at a breath. And Mr. Morgan sitting that horse, watching him run and showing me that he's watching the best dog that he's ever had on this place. He's only two years old and already they're saying that there ain't never been a dog like him. And I ride right beside Mr. Morgan and I know it sure as he does that the Georgia Breeze is the greatest bird dog that ever there was. But nobody's surprised. That dog couldn't do nothing else. He was born to run them thicket edges, built to quarter a field into the wind, and he can't help covering twelve feet of Georgia dirt with every bound.

And when he swings onto point Mr. Morgan's eyes flash and I can see something I never saw with any other dog. I can see a touch of amazement, like Mr. Morgan is finally seeing something he's never seen before, or maybe something he's only seen in his dreams. And when I look myself I feel it too, I wonder what could make a dog freeze like that, every muscle taut to the point of trembling, but not trembling, solid, the head as high as it can be and the tail arched, absolutely still over his back. When I touch him, he is like living stone. I walk past him to flush the birds and looking back I see his face, drawn up, motionless, the nostrils flared and the eyes wide, almost frightened. I wonder just for a moment if it could be the devil hidden in the brush at my feet.

Twenty feet. Not a good concrete run like he deserves. Twenty feet. Twenty feet of chain and a house to tie it to and that's all that's left of the bird dogs. Just the Georgia Breeze, tied out there in the sun getting older, like me, too old to do any work and out to pasture. Up here in this house and knowing that they'd bulldoze it flat without me and knowing that no one wants that old dog and knowing every bit of it is wrong. And Mr. Tom teasing me and saying nasty things and calling me over and telling me that his dad is going to have the Georgia Breeze put away by the vet. And me, I don't know whether to believe him or not but I get to thinking up here and then I can't remember if Mr. Tom even said it and finally I can't sit here another minute and I head on down the hill. And I creep the best I can up to where the Georgia Breeze is chained and I unsnap him and tie a piece of rope to him and we come back here. And that night I feed him just enough and pet his old head and show him the shotgun to make him feel good and we talk till I fall asleep in the chair and he falls asleep with his head flat on the floor and touching my foot. We dream the same dream and it feels like brush in our faces and smells like horses and gunpowder. And in the night I lean down to touch him, lean down to know that he is there.

Lean down to unsnap him and he looks straight ahead, like I wasn't even there, and I run my hand down each side. I can feel his muscles, strong as a horse's neck. Then Mr. Morgan tells me to let him go and I let go of that collar and he explodes, hitting the ground again twenty feet in front of us and I watch for a minute and then I hear Mr. Morgan telling me to get on my horse. By the time I'm in my saddle Mr. Morgan is singing to him and the Georgia Breeze is running like his life depended on it.

He casts out along the edge of the cotton and makes the whole loop around the field. He crosses into the next field just as we get to where the horse path leads through the woods to the field he's in and by then he's covered almost half of it. I'm watching Mr. Morgan and the Georgia Breeze is going fine. Then we turn downwind and he runs a lane to get in front of us before he takes to the thicket, and I can see him raise his head breathing in, finding no birds and turning again. And I can see that he's running hard, putting his heart into it, pouring his soul into the Georgia ground.

I am on the ground. I can't see. I cannot keep up. I run to where he must have gone and I am right. The sun is hot and I can see that his tongue is out, washing his shoulders with saliva. His head is lower now but he is still running, hunting, doing what he must. He is hard to follow and I have lost him again, but when I stop I can hear him, moving ahead of me, panting, whining sometimes, but then he is gone. I hear no sound and I begin to search. Slowly from thicket to thicket and finally I see him, standing tall, solid as a rock pile, somehow holding back his panting. Intent on the quail, invisible to us both, but there, so very real to us. And I bring up the shotgun, walk to his side, and hold the barrel an inch from his head. I take one more step and the covey crashes from the brush around me, they explode, fifty strong, ascending, flying in every direction. The Georgia Breeze swells that much taller and I pull.

Pull at the arms of this old rocking chair and think about it all. All of it there below me. I watch it. The cropland, the pastures, the stock, the house, and the buildings in the distance and I study it. I try to think where they would be at this time of day. I try to learn what it all means, what my seventy years haven't taught me. And through it all, the honeysuckle and brome, the pigeon grass, the thistles the sorghum the hardwood and the pines I can see the Georgia Breeze touching everything. I can see him moving in it all, knowing what I will never know. At home now. Running. Running long and smooth, covering the ground, running. Running like nothing else matters.

Other Iowa Short Fiction Award Winners

1985
Dancing in the Movies,
Robert Boswell
Judge: Tim O'Brien

1984
Old Wives' Tales,
Susan M. Dodd
Judge: Frederick Busch

1983
Heart Failure, Ivy Goodman
Judge: Alice Adams

1982
Shiny Objects, Dianne Benedict
Judge: Raymond Carver

1981
The Phototropic Woman,
Annabel Thomas
Judge: Doris Grumbach

1980
Impossible Appetites,
James Fetler
Judge: Francine du Plessix Gray

1979
Fly Away Home, Mary Hedin
Judge: John Gardner

1978
A Nest of Hooks, Lon Otto
Judge: Stanley Elkin

1977
The Women in the Mirror,
Pat Carr
Judge: Leonard Michaels

1976
The Black Velvet Girl,
C. E. Poverman
Judge: Donald Barthelme

1975
*Harry Belten and the
Mendelssohn Violin Concerto,*
Barry Targan
Judge: George P. Garrett

1974
*After the First Death There Is
No Other,* Natalie L. M. Petesch
Judge: William H. Gass

1973
The Itinerary of Beggars,
H. E. Francis
Judge: John Hawkes

1972
The Burning and Other Stories,
Jack Cady
Judge: Joyce Carol Oates

1971
*Old Morals, Small Continents,
Darker Times,*
Philip F. O'Connor
Judge: George P. Elliott

1970
The Beach Umbrella,
Cyrus Colter
Judges: Vance Bourjaily and
Kurt Vonnegut, Jr.